The Young Islanders

Also by Elisabeth Ogilvie

BLUEBERRY SUMMER

THE FABULOUS YEAR

HOW WIDE THE HEART

THE
Young
Islanders

by Elisabeth Ogilvie

illustrated by Robert Henneberger

Whittlesey House

MCGRAW-HILL BOOK COMPANY, INC.

New York   Toronto   London

Contents

1   Meet the Redheads!

It was a perfect June day out where Bennett's Island and the larger island of Brigport lay a mile apart in the great Gulf of Maine. Twenty-five miles away the mainland was a wavy purple line to the northwest. Beyond was the great glittering expanse of open sea.

The gulls surely found it a perfect day as they soared and coasted in the summer wind. It was perfect for the lobstermen, who remembered the brutal winter winds as they worked along their lines of brightly colored pot buoys. It was perfect for Jamie Sorensen and Eric Marshall as they hauled their string of fifty traps from the peapod they owned together.

They were thirteen years old, cousins, and best friends. School was out for the summer. At the moment they could ask for nothing better in life than what they possessed at this moment. Eric had rowed while Jamie hauled his twenty-five traps, and now it was Jamie's turn to row. A tall very blond boy, he put all his strength into sending the double-ender, or peapod, forward in long smooth glides down the western shore of Bennett's Island.

"You racing for a train or training for a race?" Eric asked mildly as one of their blue and white buoys danced

7

out of reach.   Jamie scowled and backed water.   Eric reached over the side with the gaff, hooked the buoy, and began to haul in his trap.   The light peapod rolled down until her gunnel almost touched the dancing crests, but the boys in their yellow oilpants and rubber boots moved as easily in the boat as if they were on dry land.

Eric was thinner and slighter than Jamie, with mousy-brown hair.   He heaved the trap onto the gunnel and brushed green-prickled sea urchins and pinky-brown starfish off the laths.   He opened the trap, felt around with a hand wearing a wet white cotton glove, and brought out a large, dark-green lobster, all shiny and blowing bubbles.

"Boy, he's some old beaut," said Jamie without envy. "I hope he's not too big to keep."

Eric gave him a wry glance.   He measured the length of the lobster's back with the slim brass measure, breathed an exaggerated sigh of relief, and plugged the big crusher claw.   "I thought for a minute he was going back overboard to be a daddy.   Instead, he's another dollar toward my engine."

"How much you got now?   Anywhere near enough?"

"Have *you?*"   Eric's hand went into the trap again and came out with a lobster too small to sell.   This one went overboard.

"Ha, ha," said Jamie mournfully.   "Maybe if we had *awful* good lobstering this summer, and if I already had a boat to put an outboard on, I could buy me a three-

8

horse by the time school starts. And then I wouldn't get a chance to use her till next spring."

"Same here," said Eric. He took a juicy bag of salt herring from the bait bucket, strung it on the bait line, buttoned the trap shut, and pushed it overboard. "Well, no sense fussing." He gave Jamie a mischievous teasing look from bright gray eyes. "Besides, we may just happen to fall over a buried treasure and make our fortunes."

"You and your crazy ideas! Every time there's a rainbow I expect you to start out hunting for that pot of gold!"

"I just haven't got around to that yet, that's all," said Eric. "But won't you feel foolish when I come home with that old bean pot full of doubloons?"

At that moment the roar of a powerful outboard motor shattered the pleasant silence around them, and a heavy white dory shot around the nearest point.

"Batten down the hatches, me hearties!" Eric yelled. "Here comes a typhoon!" Bracing their legs, Jamie with the oars poised to head the double-ender into the dory's wake when it hit them, they watched the big dory make a sharp turn and head directly toward them. Their cousin Pierre stood laughing in the stern.

Just when it seemed as if the lifted bow of the dory must plow into the peapod in another minute, he swung off to starboard and looped around them in a noisy circle, while the peapod bounced crazily in the middle and the two boys could hardly keep their balance.

9

Pierre took off his cap and waved it at them, and swept out of sight behind the rocky point. Eric looked at Jamie.

"He has to do it every time, doesn't he?" he said angrily. "Just can't go right by us. I can't figger that guy out."

"I can," said Jamie, stiff-lipped. "He's eighteen and he's got that twenty-five horse outboard, so that makes him a big important guy, while we're still little kids with our handful of traps and a rowboat."

Jamie rowed toward the next trap with energy generated by his anger. Eric said dreamily, "I keep wondering how we can booby-trap him. Like putting a line across the harbor mouth to catch him under the chin sometime." A happy smile spread over his face. "Can't you just see him going overboard lickety-larrup?"

"Ayuh." Jamie's mouth twitched at the picture. He rowed out of the cove, and now they looked down past the long swells breaking over the black reefs and ledges of Souwest Point, toward the vast sun-bright expanse of open sea. Pierre had disappeared, and there was no one else near them.

"I wish I had an outboard right now," Jamie said discontentedly. "Pierre can go all around the island to set traps, but we can't, it takes too long."

"Yep, and he's got a string halfway to the Rock. And he can go clear out to Fish Hook Shoal, drop anchor and go handlining for those big old cod—"

"And go way to the east'ard as far as Pirate Island to

hunt sea birds in the fall, and run over to Brigport whenever he's a mind to." Jamie sighed enviously.

He swung the peapod into the next cove, and then stopped rowing in pure astonishment. An old gray dory was just pulling away from the steep rocky beach. The oars dug frantically at the water, as if the oarsman were in a great hurry to get out of the cove. There were four

people of various sizes in the dory, ranging from a tall boy who stood as he rowed, and pushed on the oars, to a very small boy in the bow. Every one of them had a red head that shone in the sunshine like brand-new copper wire.

"Holy cow," breathed Eric. "What are you supposed

to do when you see a redhead? Make a wish, or spit, or what?"

"I dunno," said Jamie. "Where in heck did they come from?"

"Looks as if they've been picking up old traps out of the rockweed," said Eric. They stared in frank curiosity while the lumbering old dory hurried around the opposite side of the cove.

"That's one of those Grand Banks dories, heavy as lead," said Jamie. "I'd hate to row that tub for a mile . . . Hey! I know that old dory! It belongs to Mr. Fowler, over at Brigport. I wanted my father to buy it for me once, but he said it was too heavy. Mr. Fowler had it hauled up and turned over beside his store." He began to row. "Come on, let's go over and say Hi."

"What's old Fowler doing with a dory?" asked Eric. "He doesn't fish. He's too busy being First Selectman and keeping store and tending the mail."

"Well, he started out as a fisherman, stupid. And his boys used that dory when they were kids. Boy, I bet they worked up some big muscles from having to push that thing around."

In comparison with the dory the peapod seemed to fly over the water with the slightest touch of the oars. When they were within hailing distance Eric yelled in his best nautical fashion, "Ahoy the gray dory! Stand by, we're coming alongside!"

There were no answering grins on the four faces

12

turned toward them. One of the faces belonged to a girl, and Jamie couldn't tell what she looked like, she was scowling so. "You ain't boarding us!" the boy at the oars shouted in a harsh, biting voice. "We got those traps out of the rockweed; they warn't tied to nothing, and so they're ours. You come any closer and you'll get this oar side of the head."

Jamie bristled. "Now, who in Tophet do you think you are? Coming into *our* cove and telling *us* what to do!"

"We're just giving you a friendly hail, Cap," said Eric. "This guy's Jamie Sorensen, and I'm—"

"We don't care who you are!" shouted the girl. "You just stay away from us, that's all. We got a right to be here!"

"Shut up, Jeannie," commanded the tall boy. He leaned on the oars with all his strength and sent the dory out past the cove mouth into open water. The girl and the middle-sized boy stared coldly at the peapod, and the little boy put his thumbs in his ears, waggled his fingers, and stuck out his tongue.

Jamie looked after them, too angry to speak, but Eric burst into laughter, and collapsed weakly in the stern. "I don't think they like us," he choked. "Somehow I get the idea. They gave off some awful broad hints . . . Oh my gosh, if you could see your face—"

"Shut up, or *I'll* start waving an oar around," said Jamie.

He wasn't so mad at the redheads as he was astonished by their response to a greeting. People didn't act like that around the islands. Everybody you hailed, whether they were on a fancy yacht or on some battered, dirty, old boat, always waved or hollered, or did both.

"Foreigners," he muttered, beginning to row. "Insulting us on our own territory."

"Well look!" Eric gazed at Jamie with an earnestness that Jamie knew well. Eric wasn't always laughing at the funny side of things.

"Here are these kids, scavenging around in the rockweed. Then we come along, two guys they don't know from a hole in the ground. Maybe they came to Brigport from a place where people aren't too friendly, and they thought we wanted to make trouble."

They were quiet for a moment, looking at each other, while Jamie pulled steadily on the oars.

After a while Jamie said reluctantly, "Well . . . mebbe." And then, as Eric reached for a buoy with his gaff, Jamie shook his head. "My gorry, Eric, couldn't that girl *screech!*"

2 A Big Building Project

THEY CAME into the harbor in the early afternoon, long before anyone else, since their fifty traps were set along the shore to the west and the east of the harbor mouth. The big blue harbor was almost empty as they rowed into Uncle Mark's big wharf to sell their lobsters. He was storekeeper, lobster-buyer, and postmaster for the island, a big solid dark man like all their uncles.

"Hi, fellers," he said when he came down the ladder from the wharf to the big lobster car. "Think they'll have it?"

"Well, they've got the black flag flying," said Jamie.

"And the guy's sharpening his ax," added Eric. Uncle Mark's black Bennett eyes crinkled in a grin, approving their quick answers. He always asked them the same question, and they tried to think fast of a different answer each time. He weighed out their lobsters, and they had eighty pounds, at fifty cents a pound. They kept their faces straight when he carefully peeled the bills off the big roll he always carried on the car. It wasn't the thing to act excited about a good day's work.

"Hey, Uncle Mark, do you know who's new over to Brigport?" Eric asked. "There are some red-headed kids rowing around—"

Jamie said quickly, "Come on, Eric, get aboard. We

He carefully peeled the bills off.

have to clean up the boat and get something to eat and then bait up." He pushed away from the car with an oar.

As Jamie rowed toward his father's wharf, Eric said, "What's the matter, you think I was going to tell him how we got insulted?"

"Be just like you to," said Jamie. "You think it's so funny. Nope, I want to eat and get away from the harbor before somebody thinks up a job for us."

Apart from earning their outboard motors, their other aim in life was to keep from being put to work by anyone who happened to see them and decided that he *needed* two boys. Naturally their fathers had first rights, but uncles had rights if they could catch you, and neighbors had hopes. You were supposed to be as helpful as possible, and not to accept money, which was a painful rule when you were trying to save for an outboard motor *and* a boat. Jamie and Eric never refused to help but they found it safer to go around the edges of the village on a busy summer day rather than straight through it.

They scrubbed up the peapod and put her on her hauloff. They took off their oilpants, folded their rubber boots back down below their knees, and cautiously left the shelter of the fish house like early settlers leaving the stockade watching for Indians.

"Now which way do we go?" asked Eric. "Up to your house?"

"We go down to your place even if we have to crawl," Jamie said grimly. "Linnie's likely to want new cupboards in her playhouse, or something. Come on, let's make a run for the woods."

"If we had outboards and more traps we could stay out as long as anybody else," Jamie grumbled. "Then we wouldn't have to skulk around."

"If we had our engines, there'd be times when nobody could watch us. I don't mean I want to do anything bad, but I'd like to feel real free. It's getting awful cluttered up around the shore, anyway. Take those red-headed critters we met this morning."

Discussing it, they walked through the woods until they came to a gate, and here the Eastern End lay before them, the buildings set in a gentle dip in the cleared land. The southerly shore was a jumble of rocks and ledges that would be covered with wild white water in a storm. To the east the land rose up to the huge and impressive crest of yellow rock known as Deadman's Bluff. On the northern side there lay a sheltered cove looking toward Brigport and the mainland twenty-five miles away, and here Steve Bennett's boat lay at anchor.

The two boys saw the boat at the same time and then looked at each other. "I forgot he didn't go out to haul today," Eric said. "And—"

"What's that noise?" Jamie interrupted. From behind the barn came a series of rending and ripping sounds that echoed weirdly between the Bluff and the wall of woods behind the boys.

"I forgot that too," said Eric. "He's tearing down the old henhouse. Told me this morning he was going to."

Steve Bennett's boat lay at anchor.

"Hey, were you supposed to help him?" asked Jamie. "I mean, you didn't run off or anything, did you?"

"He never said he wanted me to help him. Of course I didn't give him much chance," Eric admitted. "I sort of left quick when he started talking about it."

"Somehow I feel as if I ought to go back home," said Jamie darkly.

"Listen. As soon as we get to my room it'll be O.K.," Eric assured him, as they went cautiously down the path. From behind the house came the voices of Eric's mother and small half-brother. They were on the doorstep when Eric's stepfather hailed them from the corner of the barn.

"Eric! I can use you. And bring the wheelbarrow."

At the same time his mother came around the corner of the house, carrying the wash and laughing. "I saw you and heard him," she said. "Don't you know you can't get ahead of your father? He knows all the tricks of the trade."

"Trouble with him is," Eric grumbled, "he was a boy once and he never forgot it. Got an awful long memory."

"They all have," said Jamie dolefully.

Eric's mother called to the tall dark man by the barn. "They'll be out as soon as they stoke up their boilers!" He nodded and disappeared behind the barn, where the ripping noises began again.

Eric brightened. "Hey, it's kind of fun using the pinch bar."

"If he'll let you use it," said Jamie.

Stuffed with sandwiches and milk, and munching

warm doughnuts, they went out to the barn. Jamie thought with longing of freedom although it didn't occur to him to go home. If he'd been snagged by his father into an extra job, Eric would have stayed and helped.

Steve Bennett was Jamie's youngest uncle, lean and good-natured. He grinned at them. "Just what I need. Two fine strapping bucks with strong backs and young legs. How about lugging this stuff away?"

"Where?" said Eric, looking enviously at the pinch bar in his stepfather's hand.

"Well, you can drop it over the bank onto the beach and we'll burn it. Or you can pile it up somewhere out of the way to build yourself a house when you want to get married." He laughed and began to pry at a board.

"How about us taking a turn with the pinch bar?" Eric suggested. "You could have a smoke, or go in the house and get some fresh doughnuts."

"And leave you two to sneak off out of sight?" Steve shook his head. "This time you're staying with the job. Mind where you step now. You'll drive a nail in your foot and then you're likely to be hopping around with a salt-pork poultice."

At first gloomily, and then with reviving spirits, the boys began to load the wheelbarrow. After all, the thought of a bonfire was a pleasant one—the Fourth of July was coming. They took turns wheeling the heavily laden wheelbarrow toward the cove.

"Some of those boards look too good to burn," Eric said.

"Ayuh," Jamie panted, balancing the overloaded bar-row with an effort as it hit a stone. "Know what? It wouldn't take much work to back out those nails."

"Still—a bonfire—"

"Plenty of old traps around the shore for that." Jamie stopped and set down the wheelbarrow. "Hey, how about building something?"

"Like what?" Eric wiped sweat out of his eyes.

"Like our own fishhouse," said Jamie, fixing him with an intent gaze. "All ours. Strictly private. Where we could keep all our gear together instead of having it with our fathers'. We could come here and bait up and paint buoys, patch pots, and all that. We'd practically be private."

"Do you think your father would let us?" he asked tensely.

"Let's ask him!"

They dropped their loads in the path and raced back to the barn.

Steve Bennett agreed that it might be a good idea. He even showed them a place where they could build it— around the curve from his fishhouse, where a thick clump of spruces would screen it from the view of anyone on land.

"But as far as moving your gear goes," he said to Jamie, "you'll have to find out what your father thinks about that."

"Oh, sure," said Jamie, nodding confidently. The fishhouse was as good as built. His father couldn't refuse this, as long as he didn't run out on his chores at home.

3 A Great Thought

Nils sorensen, a quiet fair-haired man with blue eyes and a slow way of speaking, gave his consent. "But you can't slight your work around here," he said to Jamie. "The first time you slip up, you move your gear back to the harbor. Is that clear?"

His father smiled at Jamie. "I know how you feel," he said. "You want a few less people on your neck, and a chance to be on your own. Well, you keep your mother supplied with wood and water, and make yourself useful to your Uncle Steve and your Aunt Philippa whenever you can, and keep out of deviltry, and that's all we ask. Sound like too much?"

"Nossir!" said Jamie, and suddenly his own grin cracked the stiff muscles of his face, and it was one of the good moments in life when he and his father understood each other perfectly.

As if the weather were with them, fog came the next morning so they couldn't go to haul, and they began to build their fishhouse. The fog mull lasted three days, and at the end of that time their fishhouse was done. As a finishing touch they bought a large padlock, and each boy had a key. It was true that nobody else on the island locked his fishhouse, but they locked theirs. The padlock made the whole thing definitely a working fishhouse instead of a shack built by two boys from the remains of an old henhouse.

When they had their gear arranged, Uncle Steve came and solemnly inspected the premises. Jamie's father stopped in on his way home from hauling. Jamie's mother and Linnea walked down one afternoon from the harbor to see what it looked like.

"I just love this little house!" Linnea announced. "I'm going to come down here and play."

"Oh, my gosh!" Jamie exploded.

"Hush. No need to fly all apart," said his mother. "Linnie isn't coming down here to play. You know that. But she's missed you these days when you've been away from home so much. I thought now that you've got it built you might spare one afternoon to take her strawberrying on Souwest Point."

In his relief that Linnie and various other small girls weren't going to camp out on the doorstep, Jamie would agree to anything. "Sure, I'll take her," he promised. "Be glad to."

After his mother had gone up, the boys sat on the edge of the bank outside their fishhouse door and contemplated the cove and the glimpse of mainland hills beyond the tip of Brigport. They felt curiously let down, now that the fishhouse was finished. The excitement that had carried them along like a rolling breaker was all gone, so they had to think about something else.

It was Jamie who first put it into words. "Well, we've got our own fishhouse, but we're still just peapod fishermen with a string of fifty pots. Seems to me that guys with a fishhouse ought to have a bigger string than that, and we could have it if—"

"*If we had our outboards,*" Eric finished with him. He slid slowly down onto his back, rolled over, and put his face in his folded arms. "But what's the use of talking about it? Neither of us has got anywhere near enough."

"Well, now," said Jamie, trying to sound the way his father did when he was keeping anyone in suspense. "I wasn't thinking about two engines. I was thinking about one."

Eric came up like a jack in-the-box. "Put our money together, you mean?"

"That's just what I mean," said Jamie. *"Now.* Of course there'd be a lot of details to iron out, because you want one kind and I want another, and we'd have to get a boat too, and I don't know if we've got enough between us yet for an engine and a boat both—"

"I've got a hundred twenty-nine dollars and eighty cents," Eric interrupted. "How much have you got?"

"A hundred eighteen fifty-five." They did the arithmetic rapidly.

"Two hundred and forty-eight dollars," Eric announced. *"And* thirty-five cents."

"Well, there's our engine," said Jamie. "Five-horse, too. Maybe she won't throw as much water as Pierre's or

26

bounce around so hard, but it's a lot better than no horses at all."

"O.K., Mr. Magic," said Eric. "There's our engine, now snap your fingers and say the secret word and give us our boat. How do we get *that?*"

"O.K., wise guy. I've been thinking that out too while you're being a comedian. I figger that if they tell us we can get the engine, they might give us a loan for the boat. We can pay it back so much out of each haul. Wouldn't take us any time at all."

"Hey, you're a business man!" Eric clasped his hands over his head like a prize fighter. "You've done it! Let's go find 'em and start talking." He jumped up, but Jamie didn't move.

"Hold your horses," he counseled. "We've got to plan our strategy first. Should you talk to your father while I talk to mine? Or should we *both* talk to your father and then to mine, or the other way around? Or should we get them together?"

"Together," Eric said promptly. "Let's go to the harbor now. My father's probably there, if he's through hauling. My gosh, the sooner we do it, the sooner we find out if we can have our engine!"

Things looked good at the harbor. Uncle Steve was back from hauling and was already in the Sorensen fishhouse. The boys had hoped there would not be a knot of men standing around talking. In fact, things looked so good that Jamie was a little uneasy. When everything fell into line like this he always expected the worst.

"Don't get over-confident now," he whispered to Eric.

Inside the open door Uncle Steve said solemnly, "From what's going on outside, Nils, I'd almost think they're coming to tell us they've set the island on fire or sunk somebody's boat."

"They do look pretty furtive at that," observed Jamie's father.

"We haven't done anything," said Eric. "But we want something."

"We've got two hundred forty-eight dollars and thirty-five cents between us," Jamie announced. "That's enough to get us a five-horse engine." He looked earnestly into his father's attentive face. "But we need a boat to put it on. So we'd like to borrow a hundred dollars to buy one. We'd pay it back, so much out of each haul."

"Worked it all out, have you?" His father glanced over at Uncle Steve. "I guess this calls for a conference. It's a pretty important step, you know. Lots of angles to be considered, and you've come at us all of a sudden."

"You boys feel you've got enough commonsense to be trusted with power?" Uncle Steve inquired. "You think you're ready?"

"Sure we're ready!" Eric's cheeks were flushed, his eyes bright.

"We've got as much commonsense as Pierre!" Jamie blurted.

"Well, that's not saying much," said his father, and both men laughed. "Why don't you boys find something to do while we talk? Maybe Mark could use you."

"We'd pay it back"

The boys went reluctantly. "What do you think?" Eric asked. "Suppose they'll say a hundred is too much? I wish they'd give us a chance to argue."

Jamie pushed out his lower lip. "You know fathers. Ours, anyway. Nothing we say will make any difference if they don't think we're old enough." He picked up a flat stone and skipped it across the water. "Of course, they didn't say *no* right off."

"That doesn't mean anything," said Eric gloomily. "I wouldn't be surprised if they said next year we'll be a year older and have more sense."

"If we don't have enough sense now we never will!" Jamie exploded. "Why should we waste time rowing from one trap to another when we could have an engine and fish more traps?"

"And make more money."

"Sure! That's the idea of lobstering, isn't it? To make money? I don't see why they have to talk so long. All they have to decide is whether to say yes or no. It shouldn't take all afternoon for *that*."

"I suppose not," Eric agreed, skipping a stone after Jamie's. It only skipped once and he started to pick up another one, then looked angry and kicked it instead. "No use getting all steamed up, I guess. Might as well not think about it at all."

"Ayuh," muttered Jamie, but they both knew they would still think about it, even if they were refused the loan.

4   The Trouble with Kid Sisters

THE NEXT DAY seemed extra bright after the fog. The double-ender sped over the calm water, and the traps seemed to come up through the water easier than they did on other days.

"I'll always have a warm spot for this old peapod, even if we get another boat," Jamie said. "After all, she's helping us when we don't have an engine."

"Oh, there's nothing like a good peapod," Eric agreed.

"Did you get any hint from your father this morning?" asked Jamie.

"Nope. He wouldn't even let me ask any questions. How was your father?" Eric rested on the oars as Jamie hauled in the warp.

"He said right off not to go anticipating one way or the other. So I guess we might as well have not said anything at all." Jamie dragged the trap onto the gunnel of the peapod and then across the stern thwart.

"Boy!" said Eric, leaning forward and gazing into the box. "Enough of them, and we could tell our fathers we don't need their old money!"

When they finished hauling and rowed across the harbor to Uncle Mark's wharf, three little girls were fishing from the big lobster car, and Linnea, Jamie's sister, called out, "Look, see all our fish!"

The three girls, all cousins, had done very well. A bushel basket half full of small harbor pollock stood near the weighing scales, and as the boys tied up the peapod and waited for Uncle Mark to come down the wharf, each girl caught another fish for the basket.

"Not bad," said Eric. "What you going to do with them?"

"We were catching them for Philip, Linnie's cat, but we have more than enough for him. He couldn't eat all these in a week."

Uncle Mark arrived on the lobster car, and began to weigh the boys' lobsters. "Why don't you girls give the fish to Jamie and Eric for bait?" he suggested. "Too bad to catch all of them and then just throw them away."

Holly and Pat nodded. "Sure, they can have them, except a couple for Philip."

But Linnea narrowed her blue eyes. "I think they ought to *buy* our fish," she said. "After all, look at all the money Uncle Mark is paying them for their lobsters!"

The other girls stared at the big roll of bills that Uncle Mark was taking from his pocket. He laughed. "Oh, I'm not giving the boys all this," he said. "Just a couple of bills right off the top, like this."

He thumbed two ten dollar bills off the roll and passed them to Jamie. Linnea ran across the car, but Jamie shoved the money into his pocket before she could tell what he had.

She made a face at him. "Smarty! Now you'll have to buy the fish anyway, if you want them."

"Ha!" he said shortly. "Let 'em stay here and rot."

Uncle Mark was counting out some dimes and nickels and a half dollar from a handful of silver in his palm. "That about makes it," he said. "Ten sixty for each of you."

"I know what you got!" chanted Linnea. "I know what you got!"

Jamie made a sudden nab at her, but she dodged around behind Uncle Mark. "Don't let him touch me!"

"He ain't going to touch you, Linnie," her uncle said indulgently. "But you keep pestering him, and he will."

Jamie and Eric got back into the double-ender, and Holly said, "You going to take the fish, Jamie?"

He glanced across at Linnea. "Oh, take them!" she said scornfully. "I just wanted to see how generous you were. But I guess you need all your money to pay your bills with. Nobody would ever trust *you*."

"Now, Linnie, what did I tell you?" chided Uncle Mark.

"Not to pester Jamie," said Linnie, suddenly laughing with mischief. "Well, maybe I wouldn't if he didn't pester so easy."

"There, son," said Uncle Mark. "There's an answer for you. Don't be so quick to get pestered."

"After all," said Linnea, as the boys rowed away, "I can't be too mean to Jamie. He's going to take us strawberrying this afternoon."

Jamie stopped rowing so suddenly the oars backed water. "Says who?" he called out.

"Says Mama," answered Linnea. "You promised, I heard you." She lifted her chin with such self-assurance that Jamie groaned and stared at Eric.

"I did say I'd take her, gosh! That's the trouble with kid sisters! They never forget anything!"

Eric grinned, and Jamie's eyes narrowed. "But maybe you'll go too, and help me herd three girls while they pick berries," he said, a menacing tone in his voice. The double-ender drifted back toward the car as Jamie waited for Eric to reply. And when he didn't say anything, but just kept on grinning mischievously, Jamie said grimly, "You'd better go."

"You going to pick berries too?" Eric asked in a deceptively gentle tone. "I didn't know you were much of a berry picker."

"Oh, wise guy, are you?" As quickly as Jamie spoke, his wrist moved and he scooped salt water into Eric's astonished face. Eric gasped, and then reached for the bailing scoop under the seat. Before he could bring it up full of water Jamie had pelted him again with another cold shower. But in the next moment Jamie gasped as the water from Eric's scoop struck him full in the face. For a moment he sat motionless, then deliberately he shipped the oars, reached down and tipped over the bucket of empty bait-bags, and swung the empty bucket overboard to fill.

"Okay!" shouted Eric, and began to splash desperately

34

at him with the bailing scoop, but Jamie ignored the torrents. He pulled in the almost-full bucket, stood up, and tossed the contents just as Uncle Mark roared from the lobster car.

"What in time are you two chowderheads doing out there? Cut it out or you'll be beached for the summer— if you don't drown yourselves first!"

Neither boy looked in his direction or at each other. Jamie rowed as fast as he could for the beach. At the beach they took out the bait buckets, retrieved the loose bags, gathered up their oilclothes, and bailed out the double-ender. Still without speaking, they put the boat on the haul-off. When they had fastened the rope to the stake in the ground at the top of the beach, they parted stiffly.

"What was your uncle shouting about?" Jamie's mother greeted him.

"Linnie'll tell you," Jamie grumbled. "She can hardly wait." Linnea was running up from the shore, the other girls close behind her.

"If your uncle was shouting at you," said his mother, "I'd like to know the reason from you, not from Linnea."

Under her dark gaze Jamie felt suddenly foolish. "Oh, we were horsing around in the peapod, that's all," he muttered. "But we were right close to shore. Honest! If we'd tipped over we could have walked in."

"I suppose that's better than horsing around out by the spar buoy," his mother agreed. "But it's still horsing around in a small boat, with the two of you in rubber boots, and a chance of someone hitting his head as he went over."

Jamie felt the dismay coming up in him to burn like fire in his face. What she was really saying was that they hadn't shown much sense, and if people didn't have that in a peapod, how could they be trusted in a bigger boat, with an engine?

"Oh, you don't need to worry, Mother," he said quickly. "I guess we both realize how dumb we must have looked acting that way, like little kids."

When Jamie came downstairs in dry dungarees and shirt, his mother and the three girls were chattering as

they put lunch on the table. He ate without speaking,
wondering if Eric was so mad he wouldn't go with him to
Souwest Point. The possibility made him glower at his
plate, and finally his mother noticed it.

"Jamie," she said severely, "I know it isn't much fun
to take the girls berrying, but I can't go with them, and
I want some berries. I guess you'll enjoy some short-
cake. You always manage to put away a good share
when I make it. So stop sulking."

"I'm not sulking," he said. "I just hope Eric shows

up. If I can have some grown-up company it won't seem too much of a chore tending out on these kids."

"If I'm a kid, you're a goat," retorted Linnea quickly.

The door opened and Eric walked in, his jacket slung over his shoulder. "Hi," he said airily. "Everybody ready? I brought my hatchet along, I thought maybe we could cut us an armful of funny-eye sticks, while the girls were picking berries. That is—" he grinned at Mrs. Sorensen, "unless Jamie's going to help 'em pick."

"Oh, Jamie isn't going to do any picking," said Mrs. Sorensen. "I just didn't want the girls going down there alone."

"Well, we'll see that they don't come to any harm," Eric said importantly. "And this is a good chance for us to get some funny-eyes for our trapheads."

"I'll pack up some turnovers and a jug of cold water," said Mrs. Sorensen. "You'll likely want a snack after awhile."

"Snacks we can go for any time, can't we, Eric?" said Jamie. He was wonderfully cheerful all at once. It was a great day after all. He didn't even mind tending the girls.

5 Invaders

Souwest point was at the very end of the island. The land here was a high grassy ridge against the sky. On the slopes of the ridge the wild strawberries grew thick. The girls ran along the ridge, kneeling in the short grass and calling back and forth to each other excitedly. "I've found a *lot!* Oh, they're *big!*"

"Look at those kids go for those berries!" said Jamie in wonder. "As if it was really fun."

"I never come down here without thinking there ought to be some buried treasure around this part," said Eric. "If we only knew where to look. Those pirates were always looking for islands to hide their stuff on, and why wouldn't this be a good one? It's twenty-five miles from the mainland, and nobody lived on it for a long time."

"I've asked my father about that," said Jamie, "and he says they all wanted to believe it when they were kids, so they went digging around, but never found anything."

"Gee, I'd like to turn up a chest of doubloons, just to watch their eyes bug out," said Eric. "Wouldn't you?"

"I see a trap down there in the rockweed," Jamie said. "Looks like it might be a good one."

They ran down the beach together and pulled the trap out where they could look it over. It wasn't really very good, but it could be patched if anyone wanted to spare a few laths and put on a new door. The heads were whole, but looked weak and old. They left it where it was for the time being, and went up to get a drink of water from the jug.

"I'll tell you one thing we ought to discover down here," said Jamie. "Something sensible, like water. There ought to be a spring around here. You can get awful thirsty tramping around here when you're duck-hunting in the fall."

"Wouldn't you think somebody would have found a spring before this?" asked Eric.

"I never heard of anybody on here ever having the power," said Jamie.

"What you mean, 'power'?" asked Eric dubiously.

"Didn't you ever hear of people finding water with some kind of a branch, a witch hazel or willow, or maybe just an alder? Honest, some people can do it. My mother told me that all the wells around the village were pointed out by a man her grandfather brought out from the mainland. He had the power to do it."

"Did she say how this man went about pointing out the water?" Eric asked. "Maybe we could try it." He grinned. "Be a good trick if we could do it."

Jamie looked up at the girls on the hillside. "I don't want them seeing us," he said. "They'll come flocking down and laugh their heads off."

"I'll go herd 'em down on the other side," said Eric. "You go cut an alder switch."

Jamie went over to a clump of alders growing near the

edge of the spruce woods and began looking for a suitable fork. On top of the ridge, Eric was shouting to the girls. "Hey, kids, you ought to see how thick they are on this side!" They went scrambling up to join him, their berry pails flashing in the sun. When they had disappeared over the top of the ridge, he came running back to Jamie.

He watched Jamie trim off the two-foot alder fork and sharpen the end with his jack knife. "How do you hold the thing?" he said.

"Like this, by the prongs," said Jamie, taking up the forked stick in his two hands, so that the pointed end turned away from him.

"Now what?" said Eric.

"Well, you just walk around with it, like this." Jamie felt very self-conscious, but he had to keep on with it for a few minutes anyway, seeing that he had started all this. He walked slowly across the uneven turf, Eric keeping pace with him. Eric was being very serious, and somehow that made Jamie suspicious of his chum. "Here," he said suddenly, thrusting the fork at Eric. "You walk with it a way. See if you feel anything."

"Oh, you supposed to feel something?" said Eric, taking the fork.

"My mother says that if you have the power, you feel a kind of tingle in your hands and the fork bends toward the ground, and where it bends with the most force is where the water is."

"Well, I don't feel anything," said Eric, walking along slowly, his eyes on the ground before him. "You sure this is how to do it? Maybe you don't remember it right."

"I remember it right," said Jamie. "You just keep on."

In silence they walked on past the beach and up the side of the ridge till they were halfway to the top. Then Eric threw down the alder branch. "You take a turn," he said.

Jamie picked up the branch, set his jaw and narrowed his eyes and began to walk. It might just be possible, he thought, that he did have the power to find water with a forked stick. Some people had it. He felt a sudden excitement rush through him at the possibility of being able to find drinking water like a magician. He went farther up the rise than Eric had gone. Once he looked back and saw that Eric was lying on the grass, staring up at the sky where the gulls floated in big effortless circles.

His thoughts stopped short, he cocked his head and listened. Someone else was coming along the shore. He could hear voices apart from the gulls' cries, and the chatter of the little girls on the other side of the ridge. Then three red-headed boys appeared over the high rise of rock that cut off this small beach from the rest of the west side. They hadn't looked up to see him yet, or Eric lying on his back watching the gulls. They had eyes only for the wet trap that showed up dark against the pale stones of the beach.

Jamie plunged headlong down the slope, skidded on the dry turf, and almost fell over Eric. "Hey, look who's here!" he hissed. "They must have landed back along the shore somewhere!"

Eric sat up and saw the redheads gathered around the trap. "Looks as though they're trying to find enough old pots to make themselves up a string," he said. "They must be pretty hard up if they lug that home."

"Guess that's why they're poking around in that old dory," said Jamie. "Nobody would choose to row that unless he was too poor to get anything else."

"Hey, you know something?" said Eric. "What about those old traps my father's got stacked behind his fish-house? They're too weak for deep water, but they're better than that one they're pawing over. Look, they're going to take it with them." He stood up, tucking his shirt inside his belt. "Hey, I bet my father would give them those traps. He'll never use them. Must be twenty or more in that pile. That would make them a pretty good string."

"Maybe you better offer to sell them," said Jamie. "They might be the kind of kids who are touchy when you want to give them anything. Make out you're trying to insult them."

"O.K. I needn't charge very much." He put his hands around his mouth and yelled at the boys on the beach. "Hey, down there! I want to talk to you!"

The boys on the beach swung around with one motion. The two older ones dropped the trap. Jamie and Eric started on the run down the slope, gathering speed on the way.

The strangers moved fast, with deadly accuracy. The rain of stones began before Eric and Jamie knew what was happening. Even the littlest boy was a good shot. Too good, Jamie thought in fury, holding onto his ear while the other jumped up and down yelling, "I got you that time! Ha, ha, ha!"

"Hey, what's the big idea?" Eric shouted, as a stone bounced off his shoulder, and then another stone nearly hit him in the mouth. The red-headed boys grabbed up the trap, ran a few feet with it, put it down and began throwing rocks again. Jamie and Eric reached for a handful of stones, and soon the air was full of cries from all five boys as the rocks flew back and forth.

In his rage at being attacked when he and Eric wanted to be friendly, Jamie forgot that fighting with beach rocks was sternly forbidden.

"Go on, get out of here!" he shouted. "Go do your beachcombing on your own island! Leave our stuff alone!"

"Yeah! Take your leaky old tub and git!" Eric yelled.

The fight was brought to a sudden halt by the clear shocked cry of Linnea behind them.

"Jamie! You aren't *supposed* to throw stones at *any-body!*"

He swung around, red-faced, his yellow hair flopping over his forehead, and there stood the three girls with their berry pails. Their mouths were stained with straw-berry juice and their eyes were round with amazement. The red-headed boys took this moment to grab their trap and make a run for it, and when Jamie whirled back they were already out of sight in the next cove. One lone rock came flying back as a kind of warning, and then in the next moment there came the sound of a boat being pushed down a beach.

Eric looked at the girls and groaned. "I forgot about *them*. They'll be sure to tell on us, I suppose."

Jamie scowled at Linnea. "Did you get all the strawberries you were supposed to?"

"Of course I did," she said with dignity. "We all did."

"All right," he grumbled. "Might as well start back home then." They walked silently to the clump of bay bushes where the water jug and turnovers were cached.

"We better eat these turnovers," Eric suggested. "No sense carrying them all the way back to the house."

"I don't want to sit," said Jamie. "I can eat my turnover walking. Can't you?"

"Sure I can. You don't have to be grouchy with *me*."

The three girls ran on ahead, and the boys ambled along without speaking until, halfway to the village, Eric started to whistle *Red River Valley*.. Jamie poked him in the back.

"How come you feel so good-natured?" he asked. "You looking forward to what we'll catch when we get home? We were wrestling in the peapod this morning, and this afternoon we threw rocks. This will be just the excuse they'll use to tell us we can't borrow any money for a boat."

"Gee whiz!" said Eric, stopping short in the path.

45

"They fired the rocks first! We didn't start it. We had to defend ourselves, didn't we?"

"That's what we'll say, but it won't make any difference to them. They'll say we didn't have to throw any rocks back, and then they'd have gone along about their business. And then they'll say how lucky it was we didn't get our heads split open, or split somebody else's open—"

Eric held up his hand. "Okay. You don't have to say any more. I know all about it." He shrugged. "They'll say we did wrong, and now we can't get the boat. Okay. So we'll wait till we get the money ourselves." He started on, and then paused and looked across the water. The dirty-gray dory was well past the spar buoy. They could tell by a rhythmic flash that somebody was bailing.

"Look at that," said Eric. "They probably have to keep bailing all the time or she'll sink right under them."

Jamie nodded as he watched the dory slowly making its way back to Brigport. It must seem kind of tough, he thought, rowing all that distance in a leaky dory to do some scavenging on Bennett's, and then thinking they had to fight to lug off a bashed-in old trap that nobody else really wanted.

Well, it ought to be good enough for them, he thought, picking a fight with us so that now we don't get our boat. I shouldn't feel sorry for them at all.

But somehow he did feel sorry for them, and as he walked behind Eric on the path, he kept looking across the water at the old dory until at last it disappeared as a dark speck behind the southern point of Brigport.

46

6 Day of Disgrace

JAMIE'S FATHER SAID the usual things about rock fights, in a calm and thoughtful way, smoking his pipe, and Jamie said, "Well, my gosh, *they* started it! And it's not the first time. We were just going to say 'Hi' the other day and they started yelling and—"

"I'm not saying they were right and you were wrong," Mr. Sorensen said. "But no matter what anyone else does, you know what the right thing is and you're supposed to do it."

"You mean let 'em push us around? A bunch of strangers coming in our territory and acting as if *we* were the foreigners?" Jamie flushed angrily.

"As long as they aren't doing anything more than salvage some old traps from the rockweed, you can't do a thing. If they're a touchy crew, just give them plenty of sea-way and keep out of trouble."

"Next thing they'll be hauling our traps, if they haven't started already." Jamie's lower lip pushed out. "Come to think of it, we didn't do so well in one place today."

"Don't go throwing any accusations around that you can't back up," his father warned him. "Most people are honest, and so far you haven't any reason to suspect these youngsters."

47

"But what if we *see* them doing something?" Jamie persisted. "Aren't we supposed to fight for our rights then? What about those feuds Mother told me about, back when you were young, when everybody got into it! Wow!" His eyes sparkled.

His mother looked up from her darning. "Jamie, it was only the blood-thirsty Bennetts who got involved in those things. And then it was mostly your Uncles Charles and Owen. Steve was always peace-loving, and your father was the most moderate of the bunch. So you and Eric won't get much backing if you think you'll start a trap war for some excitement this summer."

"Not for excitement," Jamie protested indignantly. "But if they keep on the way they've started out, there's no telling where it'll end!"

His father said with a smile, "Don't go borrowing trouble."

"Who are these children, Nils?" Jamie's mother asked.

"They're Emmie Markham's kids. She married a MacKenzie. She's back on the home place, and helping Mary Fowler tend her summer boarders, and the kids have Fowler's old dory to fish pots from. That's all I know. Nobody seems to know the story on the father. Might be he's dead."

"Remember when Mark was sweet on Emmie?" Mrs. Sorensen said. They went on talking about the old days, and Jamie knew he was dismissed. But he felt all stirred up, angry and anxious both at once. Angry because grown people never realized how furious somebody like the MacKenzies could make you. And he was anxious

48

because he didn't dare ask about the boat and engine, for fear his father would say, "Well, now, I don't think you're quite ready for all that responsibility yet."

He didn't expect to feel sleepy when he went to bed. But he woke very early to a clear summer morning with the whole thing on his mind. He got up and dressed and went downstairs in his bare feet, trying to be quiet.

Without stopping for breakfast Jamie walked down to the fishhouse, where he put on his rubber boots and oil-pants. Hardly anyone else was up yet, though Asenath Campion from across the harbor was just rowing out to his mooring, and somebody out of sight was hauling a skiff down the beach. Jamie brought the double-ender in and got aboard.

When he rowed by the Campion mooring, Mr. Campion said cheerfully, "Up early, ain't ye, son? Think your partner'll be out from under the kelp yet?"

"If he isn't, I'll drag him out," said Jamie.

Mr. Campion laughed. He was a thin, pleasant, elderly man, one of the oldest lobstermen on the island.

"Well, it's the early birds that git the lobsters," he said.

Jamie rowed out of the harbor and down along the shore of the island to Eastern End Cove. Eric was carrying the bait buckets down the beach. As the double-ender grated on the pebbles, the two boys looked at each other silently for a moment, and then Eric said, "Couldn't you sleep, either?"

Jamie shook his head. "I almost wish we'd never thought of the boat," he blurted.

"Come on up and eat," said Eric. "My mother's up.

She won't say anything. I think she feels sorry for us."

Jamie was glad enough to eat oatmeal and milk while the sun came in at the eastern windows. Uncle Steve was good-natured, as always, and Jamie gave up trying to read the signs.

As a result of their early start they had all their traps hauled (with no sight of the MacKenzies) and were back in the harbor with their lobsters sold by the time the mailboat came in at mid-morning. Sometimes the *Ella Vye* brought some interesting freight, like a cow, or an artist looking for a place to stay while he painted, or a new engine for somebody's boat. Even without exciting things, there was always a shipment of ice cream and candy, as well as the regular groceries and trap stuff.

The suspense about the boat and outboard dimmed the pleasure the boys would have ordinarily felt in catching lines and helping to wheel up freight, but they took a mournful enjoyment in the whole affair. There were no cows or artists, but two boys had ridden over from Brigport, and Jamie and Eric knew one of them. As he came up the ladder they said without enthusiasm, "Hi, Enos."

"Hi, kids." Enos was a chunky boy of their own ages. "Whatcha doing?"

"We're hanging Maybaskets," said Eric. "Want us to hang you one? Or just hang *you*, period?"

Enos grinned. "Some joker. Hey, meet Lewis Fowler." He turned to the lanky boy in jeans and T-shirt who had followed him up the ladder. "Lewis, this is Jamie Sorensen and Eric Marshall. Old Man Fowler—I mean *Mister* Fowler—is his grampa. He's visiting for the summer."

Lewis wore an old gob cap tilted over his sallow and discontented face. "Hi," he said, looking them over coldly. "So what's so special over here? It's not even as big as Brigport, and that's some crummy joint."

Jamie and Eric glanced at each other. Enos laughed nervously. "Lewis is some joker too. Boy, we have fun. I thought we could fool around with you guys for a while. My father's coming in to pick us up this afternoon on his way home from hauling."

Jamie, who had taken an instant dislike to Lewis, leaned against a pile of lobster crates and studied the harbor. Eric said sociably, "Where do you come from, Lewis? Limerock?"

"Portland," said Lewis, as if to live in Limerock were unthinkable.

"Nice to get out of the big city in the summer, huh?"

"Listen," said Lewis frigidly, "I *like* it up there. This wasn't my idea. It was my father's. So I'm stuck."

"We know all about fathers, don't we, Jamie?" said Eric. Jamie grunted. "I mean, they're the boss and everything. You got a string of traps out, Lewis?"

"Me?" For once Lewis was not bored. *"Me,* fool around with that stuff? Break my back hauling traps aboard and handle that stinking old bait? No thanks!"

"Lewis ain't used to this life," Enos explained unnecessarily. "But he could work in the store if he wanted to. He—"

51

"Oh, shut up," said Lewis.

Enos said brightly, "Well, fellas, what'll we do first?"

Jamie suddenly saw how Enos might be useful. "Hey, Enos," he said. "What do you know about those Mac-Kenzie kids?"

"Why, you had trouble with 'em?" Enos asked eagerly. "They hauled your traps or something? I bet Old Man Fow—I mean *Mister* Fowler will be some sorry he let them take his dory."

Sore as he was about the MacKenzies, Jamie felt cautious about admitting anything. "We've seen 'em around, that's all. Wondered about 'em."

"Wey-ell," Enos drawled, wrinkling up his face in dis-

taste. "Nobody likes 'em. They're trash. They got nothing. Robbie and I always fight in school, and that Jeannie, she's his twin, she's even worse than *he* is." He looked indignant. "Why, I had to black her eye last spring when I was fighting her off'n me, and then I got kept after school for a week for hitting a girl."

"What were you fighting about?" asked Eric.

"I don't remember," said Enos hastily. "Nothing much, I guess. But it doesn't take anything to set them redheads off. They'd rather fight than eat."

"We know that," said Jamie wryly.

Lewis looked around with the first gleam of interest he'd shown since he landed. "If you guys watch them on the water, and we watch them on the land, we ought to catch 'em in something sooner or later so my grandfather will stop being so soft with 'em. Boy, am I sick of being told how much ambition they have!" He spat over the side of the wharf.

"Lewis, he can't stand 'em," said Enos proudly.

"Ayuh. Well, we got to be getting up to the house," said Jamie. "I forgot to get water this morning and my mother will be mad. Come on, Eric. See you, fellas." He went off rapidly up the wharf with Eric behind him, and went straight through the village to the Sorensen house.

"When you take off, you take off, brother," said Eric. "I was wondering how we'd get rid of 'em."

"Well, with all we've got on our minds to worry about

53

I can't see hanging around with those two all afternoon. Boy, what a beaut that Lewis is!"

"And Enos running around behind him like a little puppy dog," Eric added. "What do we do now?"

"First we get some fresh water, so I didn't tell a lie." They each took a pail. "Then let's beat it down the west side. We didn't get any funny-eyes yesterday, so we can do that, and see if any good buoys have come ashore, or traps—"

"If the Macs haven't been there first," Eric said dryly.

This time they went down the wilder back shore of the island. The rocks were dark and more jagged on this side; the coves slanted steeply down, and went right off into deep water. Buoys bobbed close to the rocks.

There was no easy path. Sometimes the boys jumped from rock to rock; sometimes they had to go along the edge of the woods for brief stretches. At last they were on the other side of the ridge where the girls had picked strawberries the day before. They stood there in silence for a moment, looking around them.

"Three thousand miles to Spain," said Eric. "Wonder how long it would take to row in the peapod?"

Jamie, more practical, was looking along the jumbled dark rocks for the gleam of a plank or a brightly painted buoy in the rockweed. As his gaze reached the farthest tip in view, he stiffened and pointed.

"Look there! You were right. Scavengers been here already." The gray dory was just about to go out of sight around Souwest Point.

"Holy cow," said Eric. "They sure get around in that old tub, don't they?"

"Wonder how many traps and buoys they got in there with 'em," Jamie grumbled. "Not to speak of lobsters. Look down there below us. Asenath Campion's got some traps right in close, and they could've hauled them slick as a whistle with nobody to see."

Eric whistled. "Do you think they did?"

"I'm not saying," Jamie said doggedly. "I'm just saying they *could've*. It'd be a perfect chance. Everybody's way off-shore right now. Asenath usually hauls these on his way home."

Eric shrugged. "We'll never know if they hauled 'em or not. But if they come in with a good batch of lobsters today Mr. Fowler will really be patting them on the back, if he thinks they're so smart."

"Funny, isn't it?" said Jamie sourly. Eric climbed halfway up the ridge to a little grassy flat place and flopped down on his stomach. Jamie lay down beside him. They rested their chins on their folded arms and gazed at the shimmering sea.

Suddenly Eric said, "Look, there's Mr. Campion's boat now! But he's *inside* the line of buoys. Wonder what he's in so close to the rocks for."

7 *Who Hit Him?*

J AMIE PULLED in his gaze from the horizon and looked at the shore below. Just in sight past the end of a rocky arm was the white bow of Asenath Campion's boat, so close to the rugged point that it almost seemed to be bumping against it in the light but increasing surf.

Jamie jumped up. "His engine must have broken down and he's drifted ashore," he said. "Gorry, it's a good thing there's no real sea on yet, or the boat would be cracking up in no time."

They ran down the steep bank, across the rounded beach rocks that shifted under their feet, and out onto the rocky arm. Jamie was first, and he stopped short, a shocked sick feeling in his stomach as if someone had just punched him hard. There lay the thirty-four-foot boat, gently rocking, and no one was in it. Eric, catching up with him, sucked in his breath and didn't speak. They looked around wildly, knowing they would see nothing but what was there before, gulls and lobster buoys.

"We've got to get that boat out of there," Jamie said, his voice harsh to cover the way it wanted to shake. "We ought to get aboard and see if the engine will go. Else she'll be tide-nipped, if she isn't already."

The boat wasn't as close to the high rock as it had seemed. She lay among barely submerged ledges all shaggy with thick rockweed. The tide had brought the boat in, and now was going out to leave her stranded and battered, if nothing was done to move her.

She was perhaps fifteen feet away from the boys, and over that distance water rushed in and out with a loud sucking sound, at one minute swirling like a whirlpool, at another moment dragging out and leaving a jumble of slippery slanting rocks. Then they'd be covered again as the water poured back.

"You wait here," Jamie said to Eric. "Let me see if I can get aboard and start the engine. If I can, you come aboard. If I can't, well, let's try first."

"Heck, you can't start up that engine in the rockweed," protested Eric. "You'll have to push out into deeper water. I'm going out there with you. If we can't get the engine going, we'll throw over the anchor and wait till somebody comes along and gives us a tow."

"Okay," said Jamie, and in the next instant he was sliding down over the big rock, with Eric close behind him. It seemed as if they could cover the distance in a couple of leaps, but they had to be careful on the slippery rockweed, or their feet would go out from under them, leaving them flat on their backs when the next wave came rushing in.

It came in now, encircling them in the cold, foaming flood, reaching to their waists, filling their boots. For a moment the strength of the wave seemed to be sweeping their legs out from under them, tumbling them over the ledges to be bruised and battered and cut. But they held their ground for the moment, and when the wave drew back they leaped after it to the next place where they could gain a foothold. Then they were wading waist-deep, the boat rolling down on her side as she lay in the trough of the light undertow. Both boys reached out and grabbed for her rail as she came down once again, and with loud pantings and gruntings clambered aboard.

As Jamie jumped into the cockpit he saw Asenath lying sprawled face down on the platform between the engine box and the little cabin.

"Hey!" he cried, in shocked surprise. "Look! Here's Asenath!"

Eric stared at the still form, and then he said hoarsely, "You suppose he's dead?"

"I dunno," said Jamie. "Let's see if we can get out of this rockweed and get the engine going." He grabbed up the long gaff and probed over the side with it, found a rock, pushed, and felt the boat move obediently. He kept pushing, clambering out on the edge of the stern as the boat gradually came clear of the rockweed and only the dark clear water showed beneath her.

In the meantime Eric had been looking at the engine, and he called to Jamie. "Hey, the engine was shut off. Asa must have stopped it himself."

Jamie came back to the cockpit and looked at the en-

58

gine switch. "Ayuh, I guess he must have." He turned it and then pressed the starter button, and the engine immediately began to purr. The boys looked at each other with pleased grins, and as Jamie put the engine into gear and backed the boat farther away from the rockweed and rocks and rising undertow, their grins were wider. Eric gave Jamie a big slap on the back.

"Boy, we don't have to have anybody tow us! We can get back to harbor by ourselves!" Then their faces went sober at remembering why they were in the boat.

Eric went forward as Jamie turned the boat and headed for the harbor. He knelt beside Asenath and stared hard

into his face. "He's breathing, Jamie," he called eagerly. "Maybe he slipped and fell down or something and hit his head. Do you suppose that was it? Looks like there's a bump on his forehead. And there's a cut, too."

"Maybe he had a heart attack or a stroke," said Jamie tensely. "He must have felt something coming over him, he stopped the engine first."

"Hey!" Eric stared at him. "I just thought of something! What if he came around the Point and saw the Macs fooling with his traps, and he came up alongside and shut off his engine, and they dinged a rock at him?"

Wide-eyed, the boys stared at the unconscious man and the wound on his forehead. They could see it all as if it were happening now. The red-headed boys stealing from the strong, well-built, well-baited traps; the big boat taking them by surprise; the man shutting off his engine to speak to them; the rock striking him; and the dory escaping as fast as the oars could drive it.

Jamie let his breath out slowly. "Well, we'll know when he comes to. If they haven't killed him," he added sternly. Eric went into the cuddy and came out with a jacket, which he laid over the elderly man.

Now everybody will know we were in the right, Jamie thought as he took the boat in a wide safe circle around the ledges off the Point. We won't look like crazy kids any more just because we tried to defend ourselves yesterday. Our fathers will know we were telling the truth when we said the Macs were no-good troublemakers.

Along with his satisfaction about this, he felt a thrill

of pride and excitement because he was handling a big boat on his own.

Even though he was running this boat at half-speed, she went fast through the water with strength and power, while all the time the pulse of the engine beat softly through the timbers and planking. They were in sight of Western Harbor Point and Uncle Mark's house when he remembered Eric. He should have a turn too.

Reluctant to give up the wheel, still he beckoned Eric forward. Eric, who had been squatting beside Asenath, came slowly.

"What's the matter?"

"You take her in." Jamie stood away from the wheel.

"Into the harbor?" In spite of his anxiety about Mr. Campion, Eric smiled. "You mean you want to give that up?"

"Oh, I'm not being so generous. I just figgered if anybody's going to shear off half the lobster car, Uncle Mark can go after your hide, not mine."

At the harbor mouth the boat bounced in the choppy tide and a little spray dashed up from her bows. A few boats were back at their moorings, and Jamie didn't know whether to be sorry or not that they didn't have a larger audience. If only Eric handled her right . . . Jamie's hands ached to take the wheel, but so far Eric was doing fine, his shoulders straight and eyes narrowed as he cut her down, down, down, until suddenly there was no pulse at all, and only the sound of the bow wave. She came up alongside the lobster car without a scrape or a nudge.

61

With a smooth nonchalance that Jamie envied, Eric had the long gaff ready and hooked one of the uprights on the side of the huge float. He held on with the gaff while Jamie made the lines fast as some men came running down the wharf from the store.

Jamie's heart was pounding hard. In a few minutes now they would know the truth. Everyone would know the truth. He was positive now that Eric's idea of what had happened was the right one. It just *had* to be.

He and Eric told their story of finding the boat, and were congratulated by Uncle Mark. "You kids showed real presence of mind," he said seriously.

Uncle Owen and Mr. Campion's brother were bathing Asenath's head with cold sea water. His eyelids began to flutter.

"What's all this tarnation fuss?" he demanded faintly.

"You have a sick spell out there?" his brother asked.

Jamie and Eric, stiff with suspense, didn't look at each other. "Sick spell nothing," sputtered Mr. Campion, sitting up. "Never had a sick spell in my life. You trying to make out I'm getting old, Foss?" He glared at his brother.

"Then what happened?"

"Skidded on one of them sea cucumbers that fell off my trap. My own foolishness. I saw it drop and knew I'd ought to pick it up, but I didn't." He rubbed his head. "Gorry, how my head rings. Must be plumb empty. . . . How come I'm here?"

"These two young ones brought you and the boat

home," said Uncle Owen. "From the looks of their dungarees they had to go overboard to get ye."

"They did, huh? Well, I want to know all about it." The others helped him up. "There, I guess I'll live till I die."

"You sure you skidded?" his brother asked anxiously.

"You sure you didn't feel sick and turn off the engine, and then black out?"

"What in Tophet ails ye, Foss?" Asenath said crossly. "Sure, I turned off the switch. Thought I had some rope tangled in my wheel. Straightened that out, went forward to start the engine again, stepped on that tarnation sea cucumber, and took one long slide. I reckon I fetched up against the corner of the engine box." He grinned at the silent boys. "Now I want to hear what these young ones got to say."

Jamie was too disappointed to smile back. Eric said casually, "Did you see anybody else around, Mr. Campion?"

"Saw them red-headed kids from Brigport poking around Souwest Point in their old dory, that's all."

It was no use asking him if his traps had been hauled. He'd have known it, and said so before this.

8   *Power at Last!*

It was all over the island in a few hours, and the boys found their fame quite enjoyable. Even Linnea was impressed and kept looking at Jamie as if he had grown into a man before her eyes.

After supper that night, Eric and his stepfather walked up from the Eastern End. Uncle Steve stopped off at the Sorensen fishhouse, and Jamie and Eric went around the harbor to the store.

There was nobody in the store but Uncle Mark, and he was busy with his bookkeeping; so they selected their soda pop and went down on the wharf to drink it. The roar of an outboard in the sunset silence called their attention to Pierre, swooping around the moorings with some children aboard.

Eric sighed. "Today we run a big thirty-four footer. Tomorrow it's back to oars. Such is fame."

A piercing whistle from back on the shore made him almost choke on his grape soda. He spluttered, "That's my father!" They began to run.

"Well, men," Uncle Steve said. "You can have your engine and your loan."

Silently, Eric and Jamie stared from one calm, pleasant face to the other. They were astonished, and intensely grateful. Finally Jamie said, "Th-thank you." When Eric said it he laughed in the middle of it, foolishly.

"We've decided you know what responsibility is, and you're old enough to assume it," said Mr. Sorensen. "Of course there'll be rules, and you won't get a chance to break them twice. Remember that."

"Oh, we'll be careful," they promised eagerly, all at once able to talk fast and freely. "No rushing around in the harbor when the little kids are rowing or somebody's trying to tie up at a mooring, no—"

"No rushing around outside the harbor either," said Uncle Steve, "when it's choppy and so forth. We'll work out the rest of the rules later."

"You see," Jamie's father said in his slow voice, "it's not just a matter of taking off like a gull."

"We know that," said Jamie respectfully, while all the time he saw himself at the throttle of a slim white boat that leaped forward over the waves like a living thing.

Fathers had to talk about being careful and responsible. That was their duty. And kids had to obey. That was *their* duty. But there was one place where you could really take off like a gull, and that was in your mind. So Jamie let his mind go between wings that were made of white water instead of white feathers.

Early on a clear beautiful Saturday morning the two families set out for Vinalhaven in Nils Sorensen's thirty-eight-foot boat, *Linnea*. Four-year-old Stevie and the baby were to spend the day with Uncle Mark and Aunt Helmi.

Eric and Jamie lay on their stomachs on the bow deck, hypnotized by the gentle rise and fall under them and the way the ripples rushed endlessly on toward them.

65

"Ha, ha, I'm steering!" Linnea called.

"Swell!" Jamie yelled back over his shoulder. Steering over a calm summer sea was fit for nine-year-old girls. He liked it when it took work to keep the boat on course with the wind and tide fighting against you. He liked it when the boat rolled and pitched under foot, and you had to keep watching the mark your father pointed out to you, and the wheel kept trying to turn in your hands like a living creature.

But there was one big thought. Would they find the right boat, and if they did, could they afford it? They already had the engine. Once they had compromised on the kind they wanted, Uncle Mark called up the agency in Limerock and ordered it. It had come out on the mailboat the next day, and now stood on its standard in the Sorensen fishhouse, the most beautiful, sleek, streamlined, red, white, and gold creation that the boys had ever seen. Everyone had been in to see and admire it.

Eric suggested that perhaps Uncle Philip knew about some small secondhand boats for sale over on Vinalhaven. Uncle Philip said there were always boats and to come over and look. The boys' mothers said they'd love a trip to Vinalhaven and the men agreed that it was possible to let the traps go for a day. Once more everything was working out for the boys.

Or so it seemed. But they still didn't know how things would work out on Vinalhaven. "What do you bet this is one of the times when nobody's got a boat for sale?"

66

Jamie said to Eric as the big island came nearer and nearer. "Or else there's just one of these fancy jobs some summer guy wants about three hundred dollars for. Or some tittle-ish little thing you couldn't haul traps in."

"Wait and see," said Eric. "I'm not worried."

Soon they came upon Philip Bennett in his thirty-foot *Eleanora*, and the *Linnea* headed around the nearest point and glided into the sheltered cove where Uncle Philip lived. He was hauling his way home and would soon follow them in.

Nils tied up at the wharf. While the women and Linnea went up the path to greet Philip's wife, the men and boys waited at the wharf for Philip.

As they watched the boat head arrow-straight across the glistening blue water, Jamie thought that no matter how long he lived he would never see anything more beautiful than a boat coming home. He jumped forward to catch the bow line, but handsomely allowed Eric to make the necessary two half-hitches around a wharf piling. Uncle Philip smiled up at them.

"Well, boys, I'd better put you out of your misery fast. I've located a boat. She's plain but she's sturdy, built like a wide dory with a square stern. Fourteen foot."

It was Jamie this time who couldn't think what to say right off. His throat seemed to close up. Eric said quickly, "How much?"

"Well, she's not new, though she's tight enough, and she needs paint. He's asking seventy-five."

"My gosh!" Eric turned radiantly to Jamie. "Hear that?"

Jamie swallowed, and his voice came out in a croak. "When can we see her? Now?"

"Oh, after dinner'll be time enough. I've got to car these lobsters, and by then your aunt'll have dinner on the table."

Jamie felt as if he couldn't eat ever again—at least, not until he'd seen the boat. He said, "But what if somebody else—I mean, a buy like that—well—"

Uncle Philip said calmly, "Nobody else will get her till you boys have seen her. Binnie Wallace has her on his wharf where nobody can lug her off, and he knows you're coming, and you've got first refusal. Binnie Wallace is a man of his word, and he'd better be if he wants my lobsters."

The men laughed. Jamie was only partly reassured, and he could tell that Eric felt the same way he did.

After dinner they all piled into Philip's boat and he took them around to the harbor, and landed them at Wallace's wharf. The women and children went off on their shopping spree, and the men and boys went to look at the boat.

After the little harbor at home with its fifteen lobster boats, the Vinalhaven harbor seemed wildly crowded and busy. There were slick and shining cabin cruisers at anchor, and tall-masted sailing yachts. The big mailboat was unloading passengers, freight, and two automobiles at the wharf next to Wallace's. Binnie himself was supervising the activities of a lobster smack at his own wharf. Out in the harbor small outboard craft scooted among the boats, and lobstermen rowed their skiffs calmly through the confusion from their moorings to the shore. Jamie had no wish to be out there; all he wished was to be home with the new boat and the engine, and a vast stretch of blue sea to try them on.

It was love at first sight when they saw the boat. They didn't speak to each other as they prowled around her. At last Jamie got Eric's eye and jerked his head toward

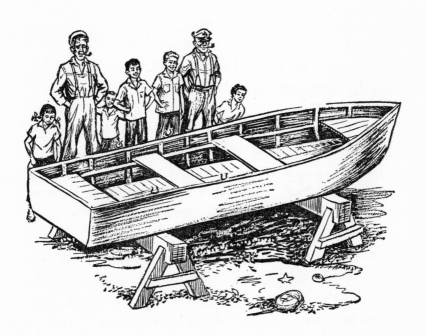

an empty part of the big wharf. Eric joined him there.
"Let's take her." His eyes were very bright and he kept
grinning as if he couldn't stop.

"Maybe we ought to shop around a little first," Jamie
said cautiously.

"Shop around!" Eric yelped. Jamie scowled at him
and Eric repeated it in a shocked whisper. *"Shop
around! What for, for Pete's sake? She's what we
want, isn't she? No fancy goop to pay for, no—"*

"All right, all right!" said Jamie angrily. If Eric didn't
want to act as if they were used to buying and selling
boats, there was nothing he could do about it. He only
wished they could buy it by themselves from Mr. Wallace, without anyone else looking on, but there was nothing he could do. Uncle Philip had found the boat for
them, his father had brought them over to see it, and he
and Uncle Steve were supplying the loan.

"Well, come *on,"* said Eric. "What are you dragging
your feet for?"

After all the build-up, the sale was over in no time at
all, and the boat was tied to the stern of the *Eleanora.*
The boys felt all worn out with the ordeal. They were
on their own now, with orders to be back at the Wallace
wharf by half-past two; so they went straight to the drug-
store where they ordered banana splits.

It was an old-fashioned pharmacy, and they sat at a
little round table, on chairs with curly wire backs. Except for the elderly pharmacist making important mix-
tures just out of sight, and the friendly girl who fixed

their banana splits, they were the only people there. Eric watched the people passing by in the bright sunshine outside the window, and Jamie read the words printed in gold letters around the wall. *Cassia, aloes, gum arabic—*

"My gosh!" exclaimed Eric. "Look out there!"

Jamie jumped, and saw the red-copper glints of two heads passing by the window. "So what?" he said, "Redheads."

"It's the MacKenzies, you dope," said Eric. "I saw their faces clear. Hey, do they come all the way over here looking for old traps?" he snickered.

"I wonder if they bring their rocks with them," said Jamie, and continued eating his ice cream.

Afterwards they idled along the sidewalks, looking in the store windows and watching the cars go by. But cars didn't impress them, and they didn't want anything they saw in the windows. Now that they had their boat, they wanted only to get home. Back at Mr. Wallace's wharf before their time was up, they sat with their feet hanging over the edge, admiring the new boat below them and discussing names for her.

"Hey, look," Eric said all at once, and pointed. Tied up ahead of Uncle Philip's boat, looking very small and shabby, was a familiar dirty-gray dory. A mast with a sail furled around it lay across the seats.

"Gorry!" Jamie said in awe. "I thought they got a ride over here with somebody from Brigport. It looks as if they *sailed* over."

"Well, they'd have a fair wind," said Eric. "Why couldn't they sail? It'd be fun."

"Bailing all the way?" Jamie scowled in disgust at Eric's stupidity. "You nuts? She's got plenty of water in her now."

"Seems as if there must be some way to stop her from leaking, if they weren't so shiftless."

"I dunno," said Jamie. "Trouble is, that's a real old dory, and she loosens up every time they hit any chop, most likely."

Behind Jamie and Eric the screen door that led from Mr. Wallace's grocery onto the wharf creaked open and shut. Mr. Wallace's voice said patiently, "Now, lad, if you'd just listen to me—"

"You don't have to tell me no more," a hoarse young voice interrupted. "I know why you won't give me no job. It's because of who I am, Niall MacKenzie's boy, ain't it? Well, I'm proud of my father, we all are, and we don't care what anybody else thinks! Good day to ye."

"Listen, you young chowderhead." Mr. Wallace was no longer patient. "I don't care who your father is! The plain fact is you're too young and puny for one of my seine gangs—too young for *any* seine gang. You put some height and weight on ye, and some years, and come back and talk to me then."

Jamie and Eric didn't move, but stared rigidly across the harbor. The husky voice said suddenly, "It'll be the same story then, too."

"Can't you—" The man broke off.

As a cold nose touched first Jamie's ear and then Eric's, they recognized Uncle Philip's dog and knew the men had come back. "I'm trying to get some sense through this stuffy young head," Mr. Wallace sputtered. "Any of you fellers care to try? Keeps throwing his old man at me, in a manner of speakin'. What in Tophet do I care about what *he* did?"

"He *didn't* do anything," cried out the younger boy. "He didn't do anything at all!" Jamie was embarrassed, and it made him feel very hot. He stared straight ahead.

"Come on, Bruce," Robbie said, almost choking. "Let's get out of here."

"Wait a minute, kids," Jamie's father said in his slow voice. "It's breezing up out there. We'll give you a lift home."

"No, thanks." The way Bruce said it was like a slap. "We don't need no lifts from anybody, ever."

They swung over the top of the ladder near Jamie and Eric and went down rapidly without looking up, ran along the side of the *Eleanora,* and jumped into the old dory. Jamie saw Robbie give one darting glance toward the new boat.

He swung himself back from the edge of the wharf. "Come on, Eric, let's get some pop."

"I don't suppose they can do much about it if we keep an eye on them crossing the bay," Uncle Steve was saying dryly.

"Lord, they're some stuffy," muttered Mr. Wallace. "Pair of Scotch porcupines, them two." In the store Eric said curiously, "What do you suppose their father did?"

Jamie shrugged. "I dunno. But I didn't figger on sitting there like an old crow and watching 'em bail. It'd make *me* mad enough to shoot somebody if it was me."

"I don't care how mad they get," said Eric. "They made *me* plenty mad the other day." He rubbed his cheek. "And I was just going to tell 'em where they could get some decent traps for almost nothing."

"Well, you can't do much about people like that," said Jamie wisely, "except give 'em a wide berth. If they thought we were laughing at 'em, they'd be likely to lay for us. Maybe damage our pots or even put a bullet hole in our boat."

"Gosh, I never thought about that," said Eric in awe.

"I hear Linnie," said Jamie. "Everybody's here. Time to go."

9 Out of Gas

THEY TRIED OUT the boat in the harbor at sunset. The wind had died out and left a dreamlike calm, and the harbor was pink with reflected clouds. The boys carried the engine and the red gas tank down the beach, got awkwardly into the new boat with the big engine between them, carried it aft, and put it in place on the stern. Their fathers, Jamie's mother, and Linnea watched from the Sorensen wharf. Uncle Mark, Uncle Charles, and Pierre stood outside the store. Neighbors were out too.

"Everybody waiting to see if we can start her right off," Jamie muttered.

"Never mind," said Eric cheerfully, fastening the chain. "We'll scoot clean out of the harbor. Shove off."

Jamie pushed off with an oar. The boat floated lightly on the clear water, and no moisture welled up through unsuspected cracks as the boys watched. Jamie sat in the bow seat and watched with a fixed stare as Eric followed the proper steps in starting the engine. It purred at once, and Eric looked entranced. He shifted, and the boat moved ahead. He turned the rubber grip on the steering handle slowly but steadily toward "Fast."

Jamie had never known such an experience; for this was traveling in their own motorboat, no one else's. Between the clouds above and the reflections below, the boat could have been gliding through space, except for the soft rush of the bow waves along the sides.

Straight as birds setting out in the fall, they headed west out of the harbor. Here there was a slight swell— enough so that the boat rose but never seemed to fall, just coasted gently for a little while, and then rose again.

They had almost reached the spar buoy when Eric yelled to Jamie over the engine, "Hey, don't you want to run her?"

They changed places, and when Jamie took the handle he felt like all the explorers, the pilots, the sea captains rolled into one.

On and on they went. Behind them the island grew steadily lower and longer on the sea. On the starboard side Brigport looked unfamiliar from this angle, and Jamie thought, What if we'd never seen that island before, and we don't know if we can land there tonight or not because there might be savage tribes on it?

To the south the lighthouse looked like an ancient fortified castle built on a high rock. No way of sneaking up on *them*, he thought, setting his jaw grimly. They can see everyone coming for miles around. A glorious mixture of the South Seas, the Gold Coast, and the Caribbean filled his head. Now the enemy were sealing or whaling crews, now Barbary pirates, and there was even a suspicion that the Spanish Armada might show up over the horizon at any time. . . .

The evening star shone out, and all at once the engine faltered. Eric swung his head around, but the engine picked up again. Then it faltered again. Eric turned all the way around this time.

"I didn't do anything to her!" Jamie shouted at him angrily.

"I didn't say you did!" Eric yelled back just as the engine stopped altogether, so that Eric's last words rang loudly in the sudden silence.

There was a teasing ripple of water around the bow and then nothing but the rise and fall as the boat drifted with the swell. Jamie had an awful vacancy in his stomach. "Do you figger we've ruined her, first time out?" he asked with some difficulty.

"I dunno." Eric was having trouble with his voice too. They both stared at the engine. "Is she too hot?" Eric managed to say. Jamie felt the shaft.

"Nope."

He twiddled aimlessly with the controls. Eric came aft and twiddled too.

"We've been breaking her in all week," Jamie said in a hopeless voice. "It's not as if we took her out brand new and ran her hard. Besides, you're s'posed to be able to go fast right off with these new ones."

"No gas!" Eric's voice climbed happily and broke into a laugh. "Look at the gauge. My gosh. We never thought to fill her up, and nobody reminded us. I'll bet they're laughing themselves foolish right now."

"Ayuh, I'll bet," said Jamie grumpily. But he was so relieved because nothing had gone wrong with the engine that he didn't really care if they were laughing. "Well, good thing we got strong backs and oars," he said. "We can always whistle up a white ash breeze."

"Want us to row together?"

"No," said Jamie, "because one of us always pulls harder than the other and we keep going in circles. I'll row first." He put the oars in the oarlocks and swung the boat around. "Not much like rowing the peapod," he grunted. "Funny how something feels so light when the engine drives her, and like some old scow when you have to row."

Eric reclined on the stern seat and waved his arm. "I'm an emperor on this barge," he announced. "Put your back into it, slave, or I'll have the overseer take the whip to you."

Jamie grinned. "O.K., Empie, I'll row the first mile and you can row the second, and I'll row the third, and mebbe we can make the island by midnight."

"Gorry, she goes a long way on half a tank of gas, doesn't she?" said Eric reverently.

It felt like a much longer way. Jamie was glad to give up soon and let Eric row. The island that had grown smaller so quickly was taking a long time to grow large again, and the dusk made the island look even farther away.

They had stopped to change places again when they heard the steady hum of a big engine through the twilight hush. Transfixed, they listened, and after a moment they recognized it simultaneously. It was Uncle Charles's big boat.

"I wonder if they're coming after us," Jamie said, "or if they're going out to look for herring. Maybe everybody's going to let us stew in our own juice."

"Well, if they are," said Eric grimly, "they'd just better not have anything to say when we come in."

Jamie began to row again. The engine became louder and louder. Suddenly a spotlight stabbed through the summer dusk, sweeping again and again across the water until it caught the boat and the boys in it.

"Very funny, very funny," muttered Eric, putting his arm over his eyes to keep out the glare.

"If they're coming after us, no sense killing ourselves." Jamie shipped the oars and waited. Soon the big boat's engine throbbed loudly in their ears, the searchlight was shut off, and they could see the black shape of the boat, and the red and green running lights. The engine was cut down to a gentle humming, and Pierre's voice hailed them merrily.

"You fellas like a tow, or are you rowing for pleasure?"

"Oh, him," growled Jamie. "Old Bright Boy himself."

"We'll be glad to ride in with you," Eric called. "Just in case you're scared to run that big boat all alone in the dark."

"Ayuh, I'm real scared." Pierre laughed. "Come aboard!"

They rowed alongside the big boat, climbed aboard, and tied the smaller boat astern.

"You better check your gas next time you set out for Cape Horn, you two," Pierre teased. He opened up the engine and swung the big boat into a wide turn.

"I suppose *you* never ran out of gas," Jamie retorted.

"Never!" announced Pierre. "Never after the first five or six times, that is."

It was then that Linnea's gleeful voice rang out from the cuddy door. "Jamie got out of ga-as! Jamie got out of ga—as! *Ha* ha, *ha* ha, *ha* ha *ha!*"

10   Whose Traps?

WHEN JAMIE awoke it was just coming daylight. Inside the house nobody moved. It was Sunday morning, and his father wouldn't be going to haul, so he was sleeping late. Except for the robins there was no sound outside, either, so it looked as if only Jamie and the birds were awake on the whole island.

He had thought of the boat and engine in the first minute of waking. He wanted to see them for himself, with no one around. He dressed quietly, and went downstairs in his bare feet. Philip got out of a rocking chair and came to meet him with a chirp and a lift of his tail.

"Hi, ol' Plushpants," Jamie whispered. He put on his rubber boots, took some doughnuts, and went out with Philip into the hushed gray morning. Once he was out of sight of his own house he felt wildly free, as if he could turn cartwheels, but no one seeing him could have told how excited he was.

He went down to the beach, where the new boat was on the haul-off. He began to pull her in, and she came bobbing sweetly toward him, as if she wanted to.

With the village seeming to sleep deeper than ever, Jamie paddled himself noiselessly out into the harbor. I'm an Indian in a sea canoe, he thought. Those aren't houses back there, they're our summer wigwams. We came from way up the Penobscot, and we stay out here all summer fishing and shooting sea birds and digging clams. I'm going out early to spear some flounders in a special place I've found for myself.

It was so vivid to him that he was almost surprised to see the engine in its green canvas cover. By now he was at the mouth of the harbor. He uncovered the engine, tilted it down, and started it. He'd never heard anything purr like that. It even beat old Philip.

Brigport looked very near in the before-rain light, so he cut straight across toward the sandbeach, then broke off to make wide circles round and round between the islands. He tried idling the engine to see if they could troll for mackerel. He tried standing up and steering her without touching her, by shifting his weight from one foot to the other as Pierre sometimes did as he roared into the harbor with his hands in his pockets.

When he was tired of that he headed eastward to where a small high islet named Tenpound lay between the two large ones. And there he came upon the gray dory. She was between Tenpound and Brigport, and the biggest MacKenzie was just hauling a pot onto the gunnel. The other two boys were with him. The three faces turned toward Jamie and stared. He stared back and kept on going. He had as much right to be out there as they did. Still the trap was held motionless on the gunnel, the oars suspended, the bailing stopped, as he came abreast of them. It made him feel uneasy. Well, he thought, what do they think I am, a ghost or something?

He looked straight ahead to show he was going about his business. He had to concentrate too, to keep away from the rocks. Worrying about a shaft and shear pins was a lot different from skimming along in a peapod.

Something clammy slapped hard against the back of his neck and dropped down into the boat. He stared down at it and saw it was the head and backbone of a bream, or redfish, which some lobstermen used for bait. Furious, he shut off the engine, and stood up to face the dory.

"What was *that* for?" he demanded. "You better be careful where you throw your rotten bait!"

"*You* better be careful," said Bruce MacKenzie coldly. "Coming out here and messing around our pots when you think nobody's up!"

Jamie was so astonished he opened and shut his mouth several times before words came. "Are you saying *I'd* haul *your* pots?"

"I'm not saying you hauled 'em. I'm just saying you better not come around where they are, and then nobody'll blame ye, see?"

Jamie held his breath. "On Bennett's Island we don't haul on Sundays. We don't have to. And I wouldn't touch anybody's traps, least of all yours. And when it comes to that, whose trap is that you've got there? Maybe you're hauling somebody else's traps and I caught you at it!"

The trap went overboard with a splash. "Let's board him, Bruce," Robbie pleaded. "Let's board him *good*."

Something clammy slapped hard against his neck.

They stood staring across at Jamie. Jamie stared back, his brows drawn, his jaw shot out. But he felt a nervous quiver in his stomach. The MacKenzies hated the sight of him, and that was all right with him, but he didn't relish being taken over by all three. Oh yes, the little one counted. He knew from experience with Linnea what they could do with kicks. Apart from that, horsing around in boats was one thing in the harbor and another thing out here in deep water with no one to see. Being able to swim was hardly any help at all when you were wearing long-legged rubber boots. And although he could start his engine and be off with a speed they could not match, he didn't like being made to look like a coward by running away.

Robbie shouted again, "Come on, Bruce!"

Jamie clenched his fists at his sides. "Let's see you board me!"

"Oh, go fry your head," said Bruce in scorn. Roughly he pushed Robbie away from the oars and took them himself. Standing up and pushing on the oars, he drove the dory away from there up in the direction of Brigport harbor faster than Jamie thought the old boat could go.

That Bruce was some strong on the oars, he thought with grudging admiration, as the dory disappeared around a long point on Brigport. Jamie found himself drifting in that direction quite rapidly, and he started the engine. He thought how quickly he could have outrun them if he had wanted to.

He wondered whose trap he'd caught them hauling, and ran down toward it. He leaned over and grabbed the stick of the green and yellow buoy as the boat idled by it. It was an old buoy, one that had taken a deep gouge from a propeller and many batterings on the rocks, but the paint was fresh and so was the name dug into it with a knife. B. MacKenzie.

Jamie dropped it overboard and sat staring at it while the boat drifted on and the buoy seemed to swim slowly off in the other direction. "That's his own buoy!" he said aloud. "Why'd he act as if I caught him hauling somebody else's? What in time did he have to act so *guilty* for?" He went on blustering, trying to hide the fact that he was a little ashamed. "Wouldn't anybody *think* he was doing something he hadn't ought? I mean, the way he looked and everything? Boy, he sure acted as if he was caught in the act!"

He looked all around him, half hoping he'd made a mistake in the buoy and that it was another trap Bruce had hauled. But the only other one anywhere around stood out clearly against the silvery-gray water, and it was yellow and green.

"He could've told me it was his own trap," he muttered. "Yessir, he sure could've told me."

He sped the engine up and darted out by the end of Tenpound and straight for Eastern Harbor Point. He felt angry, hungry, and somehow flattened, as if what had started out to be an adventure had turned out to be nothing at all. He almost wished he'd stayed in bed.

By the time he reached the harbor he cheered himself somewhat by thinking that Bruce had accused *him* first of meddling with somebody else's traps; however, he still didn't feel completely justified, but he didn't know why.

The island was up and stirring. And as Jamie headed for his father's wharf, he saw Eric sitting on the end of it with his feet dangling over the water.

Instantly his day was brightened. He stopped the engine and let the boat glide forward toward the beach. "Hi!" he yelled at Eric. "She runs like a sewing machine!" That was what the men all said about new engines.

"That so?" said Eric. He didn't grin with delight. He got up and walked up the wharf and disappeared around the fishhouse. Jamie was staring after him so hard that when the bow scraped on the pebbles he was startled. He knotted the painter through the loop in the haul-off line, covered the engine, and sent the boat out to the crosspiece.

"She runs real pretty, son," a neighbor said, going along the path to the store.

"Thanks," Jamie said sternly. By the time he had put the boat on the haul-off and reached the path, Eric was nowhere in sight.

Jamie walked slowly up to the house; Linnea met him at the gate. "Where you been, Jamie? Where you been?" she pestered. Ignoring her, he went into the kitchen. His mother and father were taking their time over breakfast.

"Morning, Mother, Dad," he mumbled, knowing he couldn't get away with not speaking, even if he did feel cranky.

"Good morning, Jamie," they said. "Did you see Eric?" his mother asked, as he went to the sink.

Jamie scowled at the towel as he dried his hands. "I saw him on the wharf and then he scooted off like a scared duck. What ails *him* this morning?"

"I think he was figuring on going out for a sail," said his father. "Got up early with it on his mind, and came up to rouse you."

Jamie couldn't think of anything to say. All he knew was that the kitchen was too quiet.

"Well, for Pete's sake!" he said at last. "That's no reason for him to quit speaking to me!"

"It seems to me you could have waited for him to show up this morning," said his mother.

"How'd *I* know he was coming? We never talked it over last night! I woke up and it was early, so I went out. He could have done the same thing if he got up here before I woke up, or if we'd left the boat in Eastern End Cove last night."

But even while he was talking he knew what they were going to say, because he was thinking it himself. So when it came it gave him a double sting.

"I think Eric would have waited for you to get up, either way," said his mother.

"Well, even if he did go out without me," Jamie blustered lamely, "I wouldn't get all hawsed up about it, and carry on, and sulk!"

"Wouldn't you?" His father looked straight at him with a slight smile. "Are you sure of that?"

Jamie exploded. "I wish we'd never got the boat if it's going to make all *this* trouble!" He tramped loudly up to his room and slammed the door, flopped onto his bed and lay glaring at the ceiling. How could a day start so fine and turn out to be so stinking a couple of hours later?

Yesterday was a good day, *all* day. Remembering it, he smiled. Then the smile went away. Eric probably woke up thinking of last night too. He probably crept out of the house just as quietly as Jamie had. He—

Jamie swung his feet onto the floor, reached for his sneakers and put them on. When he went downstairs nobody was in the house and he was glad of that. Now if he could just get through the harbor . . .

He succeeded, and walked straight across the island.

It was starting to rain as he walked into the woods. He thought suddenly of the fishhouse in the spruces. In all the excitement he'd forgotten it for several days. Gosh, if it rained all day he and Eric could hole up in the fishhouse for the afternoon and read. That is, they could if Eric decided to speak to him. . . . His footsteps dragged, then quickened.

Whatever made him turn off at Fern Cliff he didn't know, unless it was plain habit. They always turned off at Fern Cliff, and now he found himself out there, the light rain blowing in his face and the first surf beginning to kick up around the rocks far below. And there was Eric, halfway down the side of the cliff, tucked into a crevice among the rocks, staring out at the misty gray horizon. Now and then he tossed out a spruce cone.

"Hey!" Jamie called down, and Eric jumped so that the spruce cones flew out of his hands. He looked up, and then his face went blank. Jamie scrambled down through the bayberry bushes. "Hey, what's the idea of hypering off when I hollered to you?" he demanded crossly. "Didn't you want to hear how the engine goes when it's damp?"

"Nope," said Eric steadily, throwing another spruce cone out. "I don't care how she goes. Or the boat either. You can buy out my share any time you've got a mind to."

Jamie was astonished. Eric had never got *this* mad before. He felt his own face getting red. "For Pete's sake, I didn't do anything wrong! I just got up and went out on the spurt of the moment—"

"*Spur* of the moment," Eric said coldly.

"Can't you forget your mother's a schoolteacher?"

Eric didn't condescend to answer that.

"Well, look," said Jamie furiously. "I should've waited for you, I shouldn't have gone out alone like that. I won't do it again. O.K.?"

After what seemed a long time Eric said, "I dunno. Maybe we made a mistake not waiting till we could each get our own rig."

"Why? Just because I did one little thing you don't like, for Pete's sake?"

"I dunno," Eric said again. "I've been thinking."

"Oh, my gosh," Jamie slung himself back against the rock so hard that he received a gouge from a sharp granite knob, and groaned. This made Eric look around. Jamie glared, rubbing the sore spot in his ribs. Eric looked maddeningly calm.

"All right," said Jamie at last. "All *right!* You can have the whole thing! I wouldn't touch her again, boat *or* engine! You can go up the harbor now and run her down to the Eastern End, and you can *have* her!"

"Oh, shut up," said Eric, and suddenly the blank mask cracked and he burst out laughing. "What a speech. I bet if I took you up on it, you'd push me off the cliff!"

Jamie stared at him, speechless for once. Guilt, hurt, and rage were all mixed up in him. Then suddenly, he began to laugh too. He couldn't help it. He could still hear himself yelling, giving away his share of the boat at the top of his lungs. And he could imagine what would happen if Eric had said, "O.K., I'll take it."

Arms over each other's shoulders, they went weaving down to the Eastern End for a second breakfast.

They washed up the dishes afterwards and worked without speaking at first, then Eric said thoughtfully, "So she ran good in the damp, did she?"

"Boy, she sure did," Jamie said with eagerness. "She—" Then he remembered for the first time in several hours what had happened out there. "Hey, wait till I tell you! I met the MacKenzies! And I figger they want trouble!"

11 Just One Little Brick

THEY NAMED the boat the *Sea-Rover* and decided that she would stay in Eastern End Cove one night and in the harbor the next. When she was to stay at the Eastern End, Eric would take her home after they'd finished hauling and sold their lobsters. The next morning he would come up to the harbor for Jamie. When the boat stayed in the harbor, Jamie would pick up Eric at the Eastern End the next morning. That way, each of them had a chance to be alone in the boat and run her to suit himself.

As they had hoped, they were able to fish more traps. They each bought ten of Steve Bennett's old traps, adding the cost to his share of the loan. The lobstering was good, because in summer the lobsters crawled in to the rocks, and the boys in their small boat could get into places where the men in their larger boats couldn't go. With more traps out, they got more lobsters, and each paid his father five dollars out of every haul. This way they could reduce their debt quickly, and still keep out enough money for gasoline and oil and bait.

Another expense was baitbags, the little drawstring bags of knotted twine which they stuffed with salted herring, and hung in the traps to attract lobsters. The boys bought their baitbags from one of their girl cousins who made them and sold them for twelve dollars a hundred.

"We'd save money if we knit our own baitbags," Jamie grumbled.

"Yeah, but who wants to sit still long enough to fiddle with those eeny-weenie knots?" said Eric. "Besides," he added virtuously, "Betsey's saving for her clothes when she goes away to high school, so we ought to help her. After all, it's in the family."

"Well," Jamie said dubiously, but he counted out his share of the money from his billfold.

They did knit their own trapheads. It was a skill their fathers had insisted upon. An ancient skill—that of making nets.

"For hundreds of years fishermen have been making that same knot with the same kind of needle," Nils Sorensen told the boys, "fishermen in Norway, in Italy, and in India. Their fingers went through the same motions yours are going through. The men who cast their nets in the Sea of Galilee knew how to make those knots."

And Jamie looked with new respect at the flat wooden needles and meshboard polished by years of use, and at his fast fingers. He tried to imagine those other hands back through the ages. When in the summer he watched his uncles mending holes torn by dogfish in a great seine, he remembered again his father's words about the fishermen of Galilee.

This was when Jamie knew he was going to be a fisherman all his life—and a proud one.

Together he and Eric tended their traps carefully. It was always good to set out on a fine summer morning, whether by oar or by engine, but they loved the new excitement of speeding out to their string. And then there was the ride back when they were finished, lolling comfortably in the boat and taking their well-earned rest while she carried them home.

They went farther now, spreading their new traps along the west side in one direction and beyond Eastern End Cove in the other. When they finished this new string one day, they were out of sight of Eastern End Cove and Eric's house. It was so clear and still that when they looked past the end of Brigport toward the mainland, the blue-purple hills looked only ten miles away instead of twenty-five. In between, the bay was a great, smooth, pale-blue floor. Eric shut off the engine and they drifted in the warm silence. There were no other boats near them, though they could hear a soft hum from the other side of the Bluff.

"My gosh, what a day." Eric stretched contentedly. "I hate to go in; it doesn't come like this very often."

"Weather-breeder," said Jamie. "Storm tomorrow, most likely. Wind'll go easterly, anyway."

"What'll we do now?" asked Eric. "It's nowhere near dinner time."

"Let's go for a sail," said Jamie. "You know, just ride, the way we did that first night. The tank's half full. But we can't lug these lobsters around. It's too hot in the sun and some of 'em are shedders."

"Ayuh, they're pretty weak." Eric considered. "Why

can't we take them into the cove and put the crate on an empty mooring?"

They went into the cove and slung the crate overboard at the mooring Eric used for the *Sea-Rover*. Then they set out, Jamie at the tiller now, and headed toward Brigport.

At Brigport, they loitered around the harbor, empty now because the men were almost all out. They tied up at the big wharf and went up to the store for root beer and potato chips.

"Who'd you boys come over with?" Mr. Fowler asked them.

"Nobody," Eric said, trying to be casual. "I mean, we brought ourselves. We have an outboard now."

"Well, that's fine," said Mr. Fowler. He beamed at them. "Earned it yourself, I suppose.... My grandson's with me for the summer. I'd like to trust him in a boat, but he's just not used to it. No judgment."

"We're still paying for the boat," Jamie said.

"Oh, you'll have that all paid up in no time and next year you'll want something bigger. Well, that's the way it goes." Mr. Fowler was a slim, dapper, dark man with a shrewd eye. "Folks know you're over here?"

Eric opened his mouth, but Jamie answered first. "We're on our way home now," he said hastily. "C'mon, Eric."

The screen door at the front of the store slammed. "Oh, here's Lewis now," said Mr. Fowler heartily. "And Enos Pearse. You know him."

"Sure," said Eric. "Hi."

Jamie gave the boys a nod. He was anxious to get out of there. He and Eric weren't doing anything wrong, but when somebody like Mr. Fowler began asking questions you started feeling guilty for no reason at all. Maybe they *should* have told somebody they were coming over here. Just because nobody had said in so many words that Brigport was too far to go without permission . . . but heck—

"Hey, is that your rig down by the end of the wharf?" Enos asked. "Gorry, she's some nice. How fast does she go?"

Eric started to speak, but Lewis broke in. "Those little five-horse jobs don't do anything. I run a ten-horse on the lake at home."

"Well, now, Lewis," said his grandfather, "these boys are paying for that boat and engine out of their own earnings. That makes it a little better than a ten-horse that belongs to somebody else."

Lewis looked past his grandfather, stolidly chewing gum. "Of course," said Mr. Fowler, "if you had a mind to help out in the store, start learning the business and make yourself useful around here, you'd be earning an engine of your own too."

"Are you kidding?" said Lewis. "I'm out here for my vacation." He poked Enos and jerked his head toward the door. "Oh!" Enos jumped as if he'd been stung, and hurried after him. Mr. Fowler watched them with a frown.

"Mind telling me what your plans are?" he called to Lewis.

"Oh, just horsing around, Gramp," Lewis called back. The screen door slammed behind them. Mr. Fowler shook his head. "Lewis isn't used to this kind of life. He thinks it's pretty dull, I guess."

"Well, sure, a city kid would," said Eric tactfully. "We'd better start for home, huh, Jamie?"

"Ayuh, we'd better. So long, Mr. Fowler." Once outside, he hurried Eric down the wharf. "Hope he doesn't take it into his mind to call up Uncle Mark and say we're over here. My gosh, people don't think we've got the sense the Lord gave little green apples."

"I s'pose he's got to check on somebody," said Eric with a chuckle. "He can't do much with old linky-lonky Lewis. 'Just horsing around, Gramp,' " he mocked. "Him and his ten-horse engine!"

They swung down the long ladder into the boat below, and went out of the harbor with a directness that should have satisfied Mr. Fowler if he was watching. Outside, Jamie swung the *Sea-Rover* once more toward the mainland hills, instead of back toward Bennett's.

"Hey!" Eric yelled at him. "Where we going?"

"Home!" Jamie yelled back at him. "We can go any way we want, can't we? Well, let's go way out around and come home by the southern end of Brigport!"

Satisfied, Eric settled back. Now they felt truly on their own. Most of the village of Brigport clustered around the harbor and up on the high center of the island. The shore that faced the mainland was wild, with empty coves and dense woods that grew down to the rocks.

Now and then they passed a break in the spruces, where

a house showed up, and a field reached down to the rocks. Jamie felt a sudden excitement. Long ago, when he was a very small boy, he'd been brought around here in some-one's boat. He had never forgotten that Sunday. They'd had a picnic on the rocks, and he'd paddled in the water, but that wasn't the real reason they came. . . .

He slowed the boat without thinking, and Eric looked around at him. Jamie stopped the engine altogether. "You know what? We came from here somewhere."

"Who?" Eric looked at him as if he had lost his mind.

"Not the Sorensens," said Jamie. "The Bennetts. They lived on Brigport first, see? Couple of brothers settled there, sort of like pioneers—you know—like going out west—"

"Hey, there were Indians here then, weren't there?" Eric turned all the way around, his face eager.

"No, by the time they came out the Indians had given up. Poor guys, I always feel kind of sorry for them. I mean, how would we feel, thinking this was all our own and then getting crowded off and pushed around and everything?"

Eric immediately looked solemn.

"Of course they'd massacred the first settlers on Brig-port," Jamie continued brightly. "What they didn't kill they took to Canada and sold as slaves. So for a long time nobody came out here. Then it started up again, and that's when these two Bennett brothers came, see? Well, one of 'em—Charles—was *my* ancestor, and he built his house—" He squinted up at the slowly passing shores. Then he shouted triumphantly, and pointed. "That's where it is. Up there somewhere. See that old stone wall? Well, Charles built that, and the cellar hole is somewhere near it, up by the road. It's the same road they had then."

Eric squirmed around to look. Jamie started up the engine and ran the *Sea-Rover* for shore until the water grew so shallow under them they could see the clear white sandy bottom. He shut off the engine, put the oars in the oarlocks and rowed in to the beach. They got out and tied the painter to an old log.

It was very quiet except for the birds in the woods as they started up through the alder-grown field.

"See, there was this kid named Jamie," Jamie said a little shyly. "He was the oldest son. Charles—his father —got stolen by a British press gang while fishing one day, and was gone for seven years. And so this Jamie went fishing in a wherry by himself as soon as he was big enough. He supported the family and ran the farm. Then his father came back, and after a while Jamie got married. He and his wife went over on the other island to live and that's why it's Bennett's Island.

Eric was looking at him with respect. "My gosh! Why didn't you ever tell me this before?"

"Because I never thought of it," said Jamie honestly. "I have too many other things on my mind."

They walked along by the stone wall which rose steadily toward the height of the island, and at last came out in sight of the dirt road that had begun way back at the harbor on the other side of the island.

Across the road, an old unpainted house that looked as

if it was about to fall down sat alone against the woods, among a few twisted old apple trees. There was a big lopsided barn behind it. Washing on a line, a few chickens scratching around the barn doors, an ax driven into a chopping block amidst a golden scatter of chips, were the only signs of human occupation. Eric glanced at it curiously, but Jamie was not interested.

"There's the cellar hole," he said in an awed voice. Time had filled it in so it was no more than a faint hollow in the ground, in which bushes, saplings, and thistles grew thick. At one side, facing the road, immensely old lilac bushes crowded into it.

"The house was there a long time until it burned down." Jamie felt a tightening on the back of his neck as he talked. "Over there was the barn."

Eric sat on the stone wall and stared reverently at the cellar hole. "When you think of all the people that have lived in a place, doesn't it give you a funny feeling?"

"Ayuh," murmured Jamie. "Ayuh." He looked all around him, kicked at a loose rock with his boot, then picked it up and placed it carefully in a gap in the wall. Then he said, "Let's see if we can find anything left of the old chimney. I'm going to carry a brick home. Just one." Somebody owned this land now, but they wouldn't care, he was sure of it.

They pushed down into the thick growth in the cellar hole, and all at once, from across the road, someone shrieked furiously, "You git out of here or we'll shoot ye for trespassing!" Alarmed and astonished, they climbed out of the cellar hole and faced the MacKenzies. There they stood, all three boys, in front of the ramshackle house across the road. Robbie had a rock in each hand. The little one held, dangerously, the ax from the chopping block. Bruce, the eldest, stood with his thumbs in his belt.

"What are you poking your nose around here for?" he demanded. "You git, and you git *fast!*"

Jamie was so mad that he couldn't speak. Eric said coolly, "You better take that ax away from that kid before he cuts off his own head with it."

"That's none of your business," Bruce snarled, but he swung around and wrenched the ax out of the little one's hands.

"We aren't doing anything wrong," Eric said reasonably. "See, Jamie here, his ancestors—"

"Shut up!" said Jamie savagely. "It's none of their business, no more'n that ax is any of ours." He put his own thumbs in his own belt. "We're just walking around, we aren't stealing anything—"

"Then what are you nosing around in that cellar hole for?" a new voice demanded shrilly, and the girl came out. She wore old dungarees and was as tall as Eric, but that wasn't the thing that made Eric and Jamie jump, and stare. She held a .22, and it was pointed straight at them.

"My gosh!" Eric whispered. "Do you think that thing's loaded?"

Jamie stared straight ahead. "I dunno," he said out of the corner of his mouth. "Just don't look nervous."

"We're looking for the old chimney, that's all."

Loudly he said, "What's the matter, you keep buried treasure in there? We're looking for the old chimney, that's all. And I guess you've got no right to say who's trespassing on *this* side of the road."

"Oh, we haven't!" said Bruce with fine sarcasm.

The barrel of the .22 waved menacingly back and forth. "Don't waste time talking to Fancypants," the girl pleaded. "Just let me—"

"You shut up, Jeannie," Bruce ordered. "So I got no right to order you off? Well, why don't you just check with the town clerk, Mister Smart Alec, and see who owns that parcel of land you're standing on?"

"You don't," said Jamie furiously, and instantly had a sinking feeling in his stomach.

"Our mother does!" cried Jeannie. "So you git off it this minute before I make you!" The .22 cracked, and a bullet struck the stone wall and ricocheted with a menacing whine.

Jamie was furious. He couldn't bear to turn and run, all his pride rebelled at the thought. Yet with that crazy girl waving a rifle around, what else was there to do? He stuck out his jaw.

"All right," he said tensely. "Maybe we *are* trespassing. So we'll get off. But I'll tell you one thing. We never ran *you* off Bennett land with a gun the other day when you lugged off that trap. No, you started a regular rock fight, only it wasn't fair because we had those little kids right behind us where they could get hurt." He narrowed his eyes and looked at them all, one at a time.

"My great-great-great-great-grandfather built that stone wall and dug that cellar hole, and I don't care how many deeds your mother's got, nobody runs me off this land with a gun. If he tries it, he'll be some sorry one of these days."

"Ha, ha, ha!" said Robbie, winding up to hurl a rock. Jeannie lifted the rifle to her shoulder again.

"You'll be sorry first," she said gaily. "Ain't you rich Bennetts got enough land of your own to run over without nosing around to see how the trash lives?"

"Shut up, Jeannie," said Bruce without taking his eyes off Eric and Jamie.

"Come on, Eric," Jamie said with furious dignity. They turned to go. But he couldn't resist a last word. "The way I figure, it's how people *act* that makes 'em trash, not how much money they got. So I guess you're trash, all right." They ducked and ran as Robbie's stones spun over, the rifle cracked again, and a bullet struck a nearby alder with a small but powerful sound. Bruce was yelling furiously at somebody, but not at them. "I swear, Jeannie, I'll burn that rifle some of these days!"

They kept on running down through the alders and didn't stop until they reached the shore. When they stopped to listen, their hearts were beating so fast they couldn't hear anything at first. They were sweating and panting. Then they realized everything was as quiet as when they landed. The whole thing might have been a dream.

"I guess Bruce doesn't reckon we're worth going to

prison for life for," said Eric dryly, "or he'd have shot us himself."

"He's the worst of the bunch," said Jamie. "He's the oldest, why can't he boss 'em? Maybe if they weren't so busy fighting everybody they'd have something." He climbed up on a rock and saw the dory drawn up in the next cove. "Look, no wonder we missed it. There's their path, going up through the woods there. Well, let's get going." He was still mad.

They pushed the *Sea-Rover* off. This time Eric was at the helm. Jamie shot his jaw out and narrowed his eyes as if he were still facing the four red-headed Mac-Kenzies. "I'm going to go up there again, and I'm going to get a brick from that chimney, and nobody's going to stop me."

"But if it's their mother's land now—" Eric argued.

Jamie gave him a cold narrow look. "An eye for an eye and a tooth for a tooth," he said sternly. "They stole that trap off us, and it would have been just the same if it had been a *good* trap. And they threw bream at me when I was minding my own business. *And they shouldn't have waved that gun at us.* I dunno about you, but I'm not taking that, boy!"

12   Out for Revenge

THE NEXT MORNING when Eric came to the harbor to pick Jamie up, Jamie said, "Let's go over to the store first."

"What for?" Eric frowned at him. "We've got plenty of gas."

"To get something for a mug-up, you dope! We don't want to stop in old Nosy Fowler's store today and have him ask us what we're doing."

"You really going back to that place again after they waved that gun at us?"

"You scared?" Jamie's blue eyes stared savagely into Eric's gray ones. Eric shrugged.

"Those weren't blanks that crazy Jeannie was firing."

"Then you can wait at the shore with the boat."

"What do you think I am, yellow?"

"Well, you are, aren't you?"

"Sure," said Eric. "Yellow as one of those buttercups up there." He grinned, and Jamie grinned back. Eric started the engine and they went across the harbor toward Uncle Mark's long wharf. Jamie wasn't so sure himself about that fool girl and the gun. He only knew he was determined to have a brick from the old Bennett chimney.

They met Uncle Mark coming down through the long shed where he kept salt and trap stuff. "Pick out what

107

you want and leave the money on the counter," he told them. "I'll be busy down on the wharf."

In the store Eric said, "I wouldn't mind having this business some day. Be the big guy on the island—postmaster, storekeeper, lobster-buyer—" He went behind the counter, pressed his hands down on it, and glared at Jamie. "It's strictly cash on the barrelhead, chum. No credit."

"Uncle Mark never said that in his life," said Jamie in disgust.

"Hey, you know how they had those cattle barons out west? Why couldn't anybody be a lobster baron?"

"I dunno." Jamie's mind was on the morning ahead. "Come on, get your grub. I've got peanut butter crackers."

"I like these cheese things. Go swell with grape soda."

Jamie made a vivid sound to describe how sick the idea made him, put his money on the counter, and started out. Eric said, "I dunno if I want cheese crackers."

"The way you're lallygagging around," Jamie said, "I guess you're scared to go with me."

"I said I was yellow, didn't I?" said Eric cheerfully, taking potato chips at last.

Coming out of the shed, the boys stopped short. A familiar gray dory was beside the lobster car, and red heads were everywhere, it seemed. Uncle Mark was weighing a bushel basket of lobsters on his scales. Quickly Eric pulled Jamie back into the shadow of the shed.

"They're all there," he whispered. "Jeannie too. We could skitter right out by them and go straight over to Brigport and get that brick before they could catch up with us."

They could. For a few seconds Jamie actually considered it. Then he said coldly, "I'm not sneaking it. I'm getting that brick right out in the open so they can see me, and I'm walking off with it right under their noses. So come on."

Uncle Mark was counting bills into Bruce's hand, and the other kids were standing around watching the money as if it had them hypnotized. It made Jamie a little uncomfortable. He liked money all right, but the way those kids stared at it, as if they were starving and it was food! Oh heck, it wasn't *his* fault if they were hard up, was it? What if the kids were raggedy and Bruce's oilpants were so old and torn? If people couldn't make a living around here, *he* wasn't to blame. They didn't have to be so nasty to *him*.

"Thanks, Mr. Bennett," Bruce said. "Come on, men, get aboard. Get busy with that bailer, Laddie." The littlest one began bailing furiously.

"I hear Asa Campion wants to sell a dory," Uncle Mark said. "You fellas want to put in a word for her. She's good and tight."

"Thanks, Mr. Bennett," Bruce said again, quite civilly, "but we got other things to spend our money on first."

"Seems to me a weak craft like this one is quite a liability," Uncle Mark said mildly. "She might sink on you all of a sudden some day. Asa'd probably give you a good deal." He stroked his chin thoughtfully. "Or I would. How'd it be if I bought her for you and you paid me a couple dollars a week on her?"

Bruce, putting the oars in the tholepins, paused and looked at him. But it was Jeannie's clear voice that spoke. "Is that just another way of getting our lobsters, Mr. Bennett?"

"Ayuh, that's what it sounds like," said young Robbie suspiciously.

Mark grinned. "Bless your hearts, young ones, your lobsters aren't going to make or break me. Of course, I wouldn't mind having 'em some day when you boys are all grown and each on your own. Then I guess I'd be more'n glad to have your lobsters. But right now I'm being neighborly, if I have to spell it out."

"Thanks, Mr. Bennett," Bruce said stiffly, "but we don't figger to be obligated to anyone."

"That's a good way to look at things, I suppose," said Mark nodding his head. "I won't urge you, but the offer's still open—at least it is as long as Asa still has the dory for sale."

Bruce pushed away from the car. Jeannie and Robbie stared coldly at the *Sea-Rover* as they passed her. "I'll bet she wishes she could put a few bullet holes through that," Jamie said to Eric. "Boy, what a female!"

"Yeah," Eric agreed. He was watching them row away. "Wonder what she looks like when she isn't all fouled up with hating everybody."

Jamie gave him a suspicious glance, but Eric looked back innocently and said. "Are we going to haul or aren't we?"

"Uncle Mark, would you really help them get a new dory?" Jamie asked curiously.

"Why not? They're ambitious kids. Proud as Lucifer, though, and that's a fault sometimes."

You don't know the half of it, Jamie told him silently. Boy, they're practically *outlaws!*

"Uncle Mark," Eric said suddenly, "what did their father do?"

"*Do?* What do you mean?"

"We heard Bruce tell Mr. Wallace over at Vinalhaven that Mr. Wallace wouldn't give him a job on one of his seine gangs because of what his father did," he explained.

"Good Lord, boy, *I* don't know. Never knew his father. He wasn't a Brigporter. Mother is, though." He and Eric swung another crate into position. He gave the boys a grin. "I used to spark Emmie back when I was young and foolish. But she went away with some summer folks to be their hired girl, and I never heard anything more of her until somebody told me one day back along that she was this Mrs. MacKenzie, with a parcel of young ones."

"S'pose anybody else knows about their father?" Jamie put in.

His uncle shrugged. "Maybe somebody over there does. Ned Fowler might. But what does it matter? It's none of our business, is it?"

"Nope," said Eric cheerfully.

Jamie pressed his lips together and looked down at his boots. Eric always fell for it when grownups preached at him.

But in the excitement of heading down the west side in the teeth of a pleasantly bouncy little chop that sent occasional light showers of spray over them, Jamie forgot the MacKenzies for the time being. They did well out of these traps.

The Eastern End traps told a different story. Except for a few captive crabs, they were empty. They were so empty that it was wrong. Sometimes a trap had no legal-sized lobsters in it, but it always had short lobsters, the kind which had to be thrown back. There was not even one of these. The boys hauled trap after trap, growing tenser by the moment, giving one other sharp, meaningful glances. After the seventh one, Eric shut off the engine.

"Looks as if we've been cleaned," he said in an unnaturally quiet voice.

"I'm sure of it," Jamie answered. "And just a little while ago, too. Sea urchins haven't had a chance to crawl back on 'em."

They looked at each other in silence, while the *Sea-Rover* drifted before the light wind, bobbing gently. They'd heard stories of traps being hauled. They had heard about traps being bothered or cut off completely. But for it to happen to *them*—it was almost unbelievable!

Then they both remembered the heaping basket of lobsters on Mark's scales that morning.

"My gosh," said Eric in awe at such daring. "They cleaned us out and went down Long Cove and into *our* harbor and sold *our* lobsters right under our noses! Let's go back and tell Uncle Mark!"

"You know what he'll say? 'How d'you know it was them?' You can't go to the warden unless you have proof, and you have to have witnesses to have proof, and we've got no witnesses."

"Then they can keep right on hauling us unless we stop them."

"That's it." Jamie dug his chin hard into his knuckles. "We've got to stop 'em. Coming right over here on our own ground. Boy, are they some nervy!" The more he thought of it, the angrier he got.

"I know how we can catch 'em," said Eric. "We can hide in the woods, and watch, or go over on Tenpound."

"They'll be expecting us to do that," Jamie said.

Eric saw they were blowing close to the shore, so he started the engine and ran out slowly toward Tenpound. When at last Jamie had an idea, he signalled Eric to shut off the engine. Remarks made loud enough to carry over an engine had a way of being heard on shore, and the MacKenzies themselves might be on Tenpound.

"There's a quicker way than waiting to catch them," he said huskily. "We can let them know *we* know and that they better look out."

Eric's eyes widened. He looked a little pale in spite of his tan, and he opened his mouth before any words came. After a moment he said, *"Us* bother them?"

113

Jamie nodded solemnly. His heart was beating very hard. He watched Eric take a deep breath and knew his heart was doing the same thing.

"If anybody finds out," Eric began.

"They don't need to find out. This is among us kids, and it's nobody else's business."

Eric looked past Jamie's shoulder to where the Mac-Kenzie buoys bobbed. "Just those over there ought to be enough, huh?"

"Enough for a warning. I wonder where they are now."

"They set out for the western end of Brigport," said Eric doubtfully, "but they could have landed there instead of going all the way home. They could have come through the woods to watch those traps. Maybe they're trying to toll us into something."

"Be just like 'em," said Jamie bitterly. "Haul our traps and steal our lobsters, and then yell bloody murder if we touch theirs. And all I figger to do is haul the traps and set them with the doors open. I wouldn't steal their lobsters if they had any, which I don't think they have, from the stink of that bream they threw at me. Gorry, was *that* some rank!"

"Well, what do we do?" said Eric.

"I'd like to sneak out here at night, but you can't see anything then. I guess we'll have to come out extra early in the morning. One thing, they can't come up on us suddenly in that old dory, and if they're watching from the land that early, they can't prove what we're doing.

We'll lug a few of our traps over there and set 'em on purpose, so we'll have them for an excuse"

"Gosh, what an idea," said Eric in uneasy admiration.

"Come on, start her up and we'll take some across now and set them."

"Now?"

"Why not?" Jamie snapped at him. He was uneasy himself. He'd been told that trying to get even was a waste of time and effort. Two wrongs didn't make a right, parents said, and revengeful acts just spurred the other person on to do more to you. Grownups said that if you simply ignored the first offense chances were there'd never be a second.

Well, they could say it and say it, but he'd never believe it. If he and Eric didn't show the MacKenzies now, they'd think the Bennett's Island boys were a pair of weak and cowardly kids.

The boat was circling toward the first of their traps. He took up the gaff and hooked the buoy. They moved five traps across the channel and set them among the MacKenzie ones.

13   *Flying Fish*

ERIC INVITED Jamie to spend the night at the Eastern End. They went to bed early, and Jamie couldn't remember when he fell asleep. All he knew was that suddenly he woke up and there was a square of gray light where last night he had seen the western stars. Beside him Eric was represented by a thatch of brown hair surrounded by pillow and bedclothes.

Jamie gave him a poke but Eric went deeper into the bedclothes. Jamie took care of that by stripping the blankets off him. Eric tried to curl into the mattress, but the chilly air had reached him. With a groan he unfolded and sat up. "What's the rush?"

"Come on." Jamie was already half-dressed. "Remember what we have to do today."

"Oh, gosh." Eric sagged, shut his eyes, and then opened them again and said earnestly, "Let's not."

Jamie clenched his teeth and said through them, "I'll go alone then. Here!" Savagely he flung the bedclothes back over Eric, burying him. This morning he wasn't too sure himself that he wanted to meddle with anybody's traps, even the MacKenzies', and he didn't want Eric adding to his doubt.

He had a queasy feeling in his stomach as he waited for Eric to get dressed. Then he reminded himself how much money they'd lost yesterday and how brazenly the MacKenzies had got that money right under his and Eric's noses. He also reminded himself how they'd decided to hate him and Eric for no reason at all, and how they wouldn't let him take an old brick that didn't rightfully belong to them anyway.

"I don't want anything to eat," Eric whispered. "I got butterflies. Hey, it's not possible for a warden to be around this time of day, is it?"

"Oh, come on!" said Jamie.

They rowed the boat out of the cove, each taking an oar. There was a misty-gray light on the water, and already the house on the shore seemed to be fading away. There was a chilly dampness in the air, and the thin crying of the gulls around the little rock islets where they nested had a lonesome, far-away sound.

"They sound different when it's sunny, don't they?" Eric whispered.

"Don't pull so hard on your oar," Jamie commanded. "We'll be going around in a circle. And we don't have to whisper out here."

Eric asserted himself. "Yeah? Well, voices carry, brother, and this is just the kind of weather when they carry best."

"I guess you're right," Jamie agreed generously. Neither said anything more. They passed Tenpound and reached the place where Jamie thought they should find a MacKenzie buoy.

Suddenly there was a bumping under the bow. Each

boy, startled, leaned over his side, and it was Eric who plunged his arm overboard and came up with a green and yellow buoy. He looked both triumphant and nervous.

"O.K., let's haul it," said Jamie sternly. He stood up beside Eric and they hauled hand over hand until the trap appeared. Together they reached for the rope bridle and brought the trap up onto the gunnel.

"My gosh, how does it ever stand being hauled and set every day?" Eric murmured in awe. "Boy, is that some weak and patched up! Compared to this, those old traps of my father's are like brand-new!" There was nothing in the trap but the bleak skeleton of the old bait.

"No wonder they don't catch anything in 'em, if they're all like this," said Jamie. His hand went to one of the buttons that held the door closed, and hesitated. *Remember that gun,* something inside said to him. *They had no call to run us off with a gun.* He turned both buttons, flipped the door open, and slid the trap off the gunnel. They let the warp go after it, and threw the buoy after that.

He knew where the next one was now, so he rowed and Eric again caught the buoy. But when Jamie swung the bow around not toward Bennett's, but toward the passage between Brigport and Tenpound, Eric was uneasy again.

"Two ought to be enough warning," he muttered.

"How many of our good traps did they haul yesterday?"

"Ten."

"Then we haul ten of theirs. Even then, it's more than fair because we had lobsters in *our* traps and there'll likely be no more in the other eight of theirs than there were in the first two. If any of 'em *do* have a lobster," he conceded, "we won't take it."

"My gosh, no!" Eric looked shocked.

Between MacKenzie pots, they hauled their own which they'd brought over yesterday. By the time they'd finished the entire job the morning was much lighter, and they both felt as if dozens of eyes watched them from the shelter of woods and rocks on the Brigport shore. Jamie half expected to hear a bullet go by them or even hit the side of the boat. But they saw nothing and heard nothing except the usual gull noises and the sounds of engines starting up in both harbors.

Once within hailing distance of their own woods, Eric breathed a gusty sigh of relief. Jamie, though he wouldn't admit, was also relieved. Now they felt ravenously hungry, so they headed into the cove, and went up to the house without lingering.

Everyone was up now and the kitchen smelled of good food. "Where've you fellas been?" Uncle Steve asked them.

"Oh, out rowing around," said Eric, and began to play with the baby in her high chair. Jamie offered to tie little Stevie's shoe laces for him. Nobody asked any more questions.

After breakfast, they hauled what traps they had left outside the cove, then went down past the harbor and hauled the traps on the west side. They did well out of them.

However, there were always places that weren't very productive, and the boys picked out five traps that hadn't been fishing well and loaded them in careful balance aboard the *Sea-Rover*. They went back to the harbor, running slowly. Eric, who was steering, had to turn the *Sea-Rover's* nose twice into the wake of the big boats to keep her from rolling wildly with her load of pots.

After they sold their lobsters, they took the five pots back down to the Eastern End to replace the five traps which they'd scattered among the MacKenzie string. The morning mists were burning away now as the sun rose high, but it shone on no red heads and gray dory against the Brigport shore.

Eric shut off the engine and said, "Looks as if the Macs are late getting out to haul this morning."

"Maybe they're hauling their other string first," said Jamie. "They've got some on the back side of Brigport. I saw them that day."

"Maybe they've already found their traps hauled, and nothing in ours, so they've gone home to think it over, and this'll be the end of it," Eric suggested.

Jamie grunted. "It'll be the end of it unless they set *ours* with the doors open. Let's check 'em."

Eric started up the engine and headed down past Eastern End Cove on their right and then past Tenpound on their left, toward the farthest buoy in that string. Jamie gaffed the buoy and Eric shut off the engine. They were utterly absorbed in watching eagerly to see if the trap would come up with an open door.

They didn't see or hear anything else then until an

enormous splash sounded behind them. They jumped so that the wet warp flew out of their hands and the trap slid back to bottom, while the boat rocked wildly. They swung around just in time to see wet traps being pushed off the MacKenzies' dory, five of them one after another, right on top of each other. It looked at first as if there were ten red heads in the dory, and at least twenty pairs of hands flinging out a wild tangle of warps and blue-and-white buoys—*Jamie's and Eric's buoys.* They floated on the water like a cluster of some new kind of water lilies.

Bruce MacKenzie stood up in the bow of the dory, his thumbs under the bib of his tattered oilpants, and his teeth flashed as he laughed at them. "If you can sort out that snarl you're real smart even for numbhead Sorensens and Bennetts! Anyway, that'll learn ye not to come crowding into MacKenzie territory!"

Robbie leaned out by him and thumbed his nose. Small Laddie waggled his hands at his ears, stuck out his tongue, and yelled, "Ya! Ya! Ya!" Jeannie sat in the stern, smiling scornfully.

Jamie and Eric got their breath. They realized at once that the MacKenzies must have been hiding behind Tenpound on the chance that they'd be back.

"So what'll learn *you* not to haul other people's pots?" Jamie shouted back.

"Who said we did?"

"*I* said so! I saw what you sold yesterday! You never got those out of *your* pots, old as they are and with that stinking bait!"

"How come you know what my pots look like?" Bruce

demanded. "I reckon the warden'd be interested in that!"

"Look who's talking about the warden!" Eric hooted.

"Ayuh, look!" Bruce mocked him. "What were you doing out at dawn this morning?"

"Who said we were?"

"Had to be you. There were your five traps, and there were ours set with the doors open. You think we're stupid as well as shiftless?"

"I sure do!" Eric yelled back. Slow to anger, Eric was now good and mad. Jamie was staring with burning eyes at the cluster of blue and white buoys floating on the water. It would be practically impossible to unsnarl the warps. They couldn't haul up all five traps together in one huge unwieldy bundle, and so they'd be a total loss. Five strong new traps with nylon heads and new rope, each one costing six or seven dollars to build and set. So there went thirty dollars or so to the bottom of the sea.

He reached down into the bait bucket, took out a full baitbag, and hurled it straight at Bruce. It caught him in the face with a satisfying, juicy *plop*.

Bruce, coughing, spitting, and swearing, grabbed up the baitbag where it fell at his feet, and slung it back. Dodging, the boys almost fell overboard. It hit Eric a wet smack on the shoulder, and he picked it up and threw it. This time it caught Robbie, who yelled in outrage and scrambled around in the bottom of the dory and came up with a bream in each hand. All the time the *Sea-Rover* was drifting toward the land, and the dory was drifting down on her.

The bream went sailing through the air, but fell short and went into the water. However, the baitbag came back and caught Jamie on the ear. Jeannie grabbed an oar and was paddling the dory so that it kept gaining on the drifting *Sea-Rover*. In fact it gained so fast that Robbie's next bream slapped Eric across the face and he flung it back. Laddie got it and began to howl.

"Hit my little brother, will you?" Jeannie shrieked.

"Why don't you keep him home?" Eric yelled at her. "And *you* stay home where you belong!" This was broken off by the return of the full baitbag, which seemed to get juicier and messier each time it struck.

Eric wiped his arm across his mouth, seized two more full baitbags from the bucket and lobbed first one and then the other into the enemy galley. Now the dory loomed very close. She was much higher and longer than the *Sea-Rover*. By pure luck Eric's missiles caught Bruce off balance, so he stumbled backward in the dory and bumped into the fiercely prancing Robbie and knocked him over a seat. Laddie's howls rose to heaven. Only Jeannie kept a sort of savage composure, poling the dory down on the smaller boat as if she intended to ram and sink it.

In the confusion Jamie started the engine and ran for the nearest shore—a line of rock below the woods that hid the house and the cove.

"If we get in there and have the woods behind us we can drive 'em off!" he shouted to Eric. "This way we have to keep running so that darn female can't board us with that oar!"

All the time the *Sea-Rover* was drifting toward land.

Eric nodded. He stood amidships, a baitbag in one hand and a bream in the other, waiting for the targets in the dory to sort themselves out. His eyes were blazing, his cheeks red under the smears of herring blood and grease and scales.

"This is a swell fight!" he announced. "I hope nobody comes along and spoils it!"

Jamie grinned. "I just wish they'd left that little kid and that girl at home!"

The *Sea-Rover* went in between two boulders and grounded out on underwater rocks, and Jamie shut off and tilted up the engine. The two boys bounded overboard in their rubber boots, dragged the boat behind them up onto a flat slant of rock, and took out what was left of their ammunition. In addition they grabbed handfuls of wet cold rockweed pulled off the rocks, and clods of the dry, scratchy earth at the edge of the woods.

"Don't fire till you see the whites of their eyes," Jamie ordered tensely. They waited until the dory was almost ready to ground, and then let go with a barrage. It was successful at first. It kept the MacKenzies from landing. Hurling epithets like rocks, they shipped their oars and began hurling bream. On solid ground at last, Jamie and Eric could concentrate on throwing too, and the air was full of flying missiles and insults that echoed wildly from the woods.

A yelp from Jeannie meant that a swatch of icy-cold wet rockweed had caught her in the face, and Jamie howled in delight to watch her clawing it off. In a fury she threw the bailing scoop, which Jamie dodged, and it flew apart when it hit the rocks.

"*Now* how'll you get home?" he shouted. "Have to bail with your shoe unless that's full of holes like your dory!"

Into this scene of havoc came Steve Bennett's boat *Philippa*. White and beautiful, she came out past the point that had safely hidden them from the cove. Eric's jaw dropped, and a hunk of turf dropped from one hand, a bream from the other. Robbie seized the moment to aim a baitbag which caught Eric in the midriff. Eric doubled, but continued to stare at his father's boat as if she were the *Flying Dutchman*, and then Jamie saw her. The MacKenzies turned and looked too.

Steve had seen them. Her engine pulsing softly in the sudden silence, the *Philippa* headed in toward shore at a lazy rate. The four in the dory dropped their weapons as the two on the shore had done. While the younger ones stared as if they too saw a ghost ship, Bruce fumbled with slippery hands to get the oars between the tholepins.

Steve swung the boat around broadside to the shore. Philippa sat on the engine box with the baby in her arms and young Steve beside her. "What's going on, boys?" Uncle Steve called pleasantly.

"Nothing," Eric called back, sublimely ignoring the fact that he was a mess.

"Nothing, huh?" Steve nodded at the MacKenzies. "That what you call it, Bruce? What are you doing, airing that bait or drying it out?"

"We're just talking," said Bruce.

"Some conversation, from what I heard of it back in the cove. Real loud. Interesting, too. I didn't know you fellas knew so many words." His casual dark gaze took them all in, then fixed definitely on Jamie and Eric. "Supposing you two come aboard and go over to Brigport with me. We'll take the boat in tow."

"Like *this?*" demanded Eric, pointing righteously to his soaked shirt and smeared face.

"Salt water'll take care of your skin and hair. And we'll just have to stand the rest. Get aboard."

The MacKenzies never spoke a word from the dory, but that didn't mean they couldn't be laughing their heads off inside at seeing Jamie and Eric called away like a couple of little kids.

"We're going to have that fight some day," Jamie muttered through his teeth as they launched the boat. "We've *got* to have it, right clean through to the end."

"You bet," Eric muttered back. They didn't look at the MacKenzies as they poled out past the dory, and the MacKenzies didn't speak. Jamie realized belatedly that the MacKenzies wanted to keep the fight quiet, too. They hadn't told Steve that the boys had been meddling with their traps, and they could have. He stole a glance at them then, and met Jeannie's ferocious grin.

"Just you wait," she mouthed.

"Just *you* wait." He shaped the words with a fearful grimace.

14   Lewis the Listener

As the *Philippa* speeded up and left the dory behind, Steve summoned the boys up beside the wheel with a lift of his chin. "All right, what was going on back there?"

"Nothing, I told you," said Eric politely.

"Looked like quite a bit of something to me." He glanced sidewise at Jamie. "What do *you* say?"

"Nothing," said Jamie, also being very polite.

Steve nodded. "We'll get to this sooner or later. If you don't want to talk about it now, you'll have to sometime. Don't forget that. Now you'd better wash."

Eric's mother gave them a clean diaper to wash with, and they took turns soaking it in cold sea water and scrubbing their faces, ears, and heads.

They reached Brigport as the mailboat came in, and there was a small crowd on the wharf. Steve tied up at the machine shop wharf, and his wife took the children to call on a friend. Jamie and Eric were on their own. Though they were uneasy about the inevitable discussion with their fathers, they could always eat; so they picked up some pop and potato chips at the store, and then went down onto the boat wharf.

Now that they'd cooled off from the excitement, they sat down on the warm splintery planks and drank their cold root beer while the donkey engine coughed and chugged, and the hoisting mast creaked, and lumber was swung out and up and onto the wharf. Lewis Fowler and Enos Pearse leaned against the spilings, watching.

After a moment they came and sprawled on the planks beside Jamie and Eric, each accepted a turn at the pop bottle, and exchanged a few remarks. Enos wanted to know more about the new engine. "I'll have one next year," he said enviously, "but it won't be any measly old five-horse."

"You think your mother will trust you with a ten-horse when she doesn't even trust you rowing now?" inquired Jamie.

"Hard to tell," Enos admitted.

"Hey, look," Lewis said, "somebody's woodbox got adrift!"

Grinning broadly, he pointed down the harbor, and they saw the MacKenzie dory coming slowly among the moorings.

"Boy, I wish I had my air rifle right here to pepper them!"

"Ayuh," Enos agreed. "Bet they'd feel as if they'd fell into a hornet's nest."

At the sight of the dory and the redheads, Jamie and Eric felt their resentment of the MacKenzies rising like the spring flood tides. But they hid it from the other boys.

Lewis watched the dory come, a self-satisfied smile curling his mouth. "You wait till they get close enough.

I'll yell, 'Hey, where's your father?' and you just watch what happens then."

Jamie could tell by the way Eric looked down at the toes of his boots that he was uneasy. There was no telling about Eric. His face looked closed up somehow, and that made Jamie uneasy too.

"Well, where is their father?" Eric said, still looking down.

"In jail," said Lewis triumphantly. "In Connecticut. I guess for life, but I'm not sure. But I know he killed somebody."

Jamie and Eric stared at him. Jamie felt a curious sensation in his stomach, like a fist suddenly closing up tight. The taste of root beer in his mouth was suddenly so bitter he wanted to spit.

"See, Lewis knows all about it," Enos said proudly. "And he told me. His grandfather's First Selectman, and Lewis heard him and the others having a meeting in the kitchen last week."

Lewis smiled modestly. "I was s'posed to be asleep. I went down the back stairs and listened."

"Tell 'em the rest of it," Enos urged him.

"Well, see," said Lewis. "His father killed somebody where he worked, and his mother didn't have any way to support the kids so she brought 'em all back here. Guess she thought she could move into the old home place, and the kids could go lobstering as soon as they were old enough." He stared out at the approaching dory, and his mouth twisted.

"Look at 'em! Have to have the town feed 'em. I heard all about that when I was listening on the back stairs!"

Eric and Jamie looked at him solemnly, not even blinking.

"Sure, they're on the town," Lewis went on scornfully. "And their mother helps out my grandmother with her summer boarders. I heard the selectmen talking the other night, trying to decide whether it would be cheaper to pay Bruce's tuition to high school on the mainland or get him a decent boat so he can really fish some traps and start supporting the family." He snorted. "He won't take anything, though. He's so stuck on himself it all but turns his stomach to get grub in the store."

He's not too proud to haul our traps, though, Jamie thought. Aloud he said, "They ever do anything around here like stealing, or shooting out people's windows, or anything like that?"

Lewis shrugged. "I dunno. I never heard," he said indifferently. The dory was very close now, they could see clearly the faces of the younger children turned with wonder and interest toward the mailboat. When they weren't fighting they looked just like anybody else. Jeannie leaned forward and said something to the little boy, and pointed at the gull perched on the *Ella's* mast. They were both smiling.

"They've run us off their place once this summer," Enos said. "All we wanted was to see what they had up there. We never touched anything, just looked in the windows when we thought they weren't home, and—"

"Oh, shut up," said Lewis menacingly. "You know what I told you. If anything ever gets back to my grandfather I'll be a dead duck, and I'll see that you're one too."

"I never told anybody anything," Enos protested.

"Well, you're sure talking now," said Lewis. He got up and walked down to the far end of the deserted wharf. Enos jumped up and followed him, and Eric and Jamie, glancing at each other, got up and went too. The dory was just edging up to the foot of the ladder.

"Hey," Lewis called softly. "Heard from your father lately?" The four faces turned up instantly and stared at the four faces looking down from the wharf.

Then Bruce said just as softly, "I'll kill you, Lewis Fowler, I'll slit your throat just as sure as you're born."

"Then that'll be two of you in jail," said Lewis.

Jamie felt again, without warning, the fist clenching shut in his stomach. He felt a movement close to him, looked around and saw Eric walking away up the wharf. Jamie followed him. Behind them they heard Enos. "Hey, what you got in that old shack up there that you don't want anybody looking at?"

Jamie and Eric walked a little faster. When they were a good distance away from everyone Jamie muttered, "Just the same, they shouldn't have hauled our traps. And throwing rocks at us on our own land when we didn't start it. And that gun—"

"Ayuh, I know, I know," Eric interrupted, and they glared at each other and went the rest of the way around the harbor to the *Philippa* in silence.

133

15   *Time to Think*

It was Jamie's turn to keep the *Sea-Rover* overnight, so he went alone from the Eastern End to the harbor.   Uncle Steve had been the same as always, but that didn't mean he'd forgotten what he'd promised aboard the *Philippa*.   So that was one reason for Jamie to miss the usual exhilaration he felt when he was alone in the *Sea-Rover*—but today it wasn't the only reason. When he landed, he stopped where the double-ender was overturned on the dry turf, covered with an old canvas sprayhood to keep her from drying out in the sun.

He and Eric had talked about selling the double-ender. Jamie hated to; he felt as if she were a dear old horse. But still she was meant for the water, and both boys felt she should be on it instead of useless on the beach.   Uncle Philip was going to mention her around on Vinalhaven in case some man wanted a good peapod for his boy.

After Jamie looked at her for a few minutes, he replaced the sprayhood and went home.   His father had gone to haul, but his mother and Linnea were as glad to see him as if he'd been gone a week instead of only since last night.

"Goodness, what happened to your shirt?" his mother asked after the greetings.

"Nothing," said Jamie.   "I'll change it before I eat."

"I don't know what you'd do without the word *nothing*," said his mother.

You'll know it's more than nothing as soon as Uncle Steve talks to Dad, he thought glumly. Maybe I better tell him first. . . . But he wasn't as worried about that as he should have been. There was something else on his mind which he couldn't put into words, even to himself.

After dinner he got fresh water. Since there was nothing more his mother wanted done, he set out for the Eastern End on foot. Every so often he sighed. He felt very odd. It wasn't a sick or an unhappy feeling, but then neither was it a springy, alert, ready-for-what-comes-next feeling. He didn't like it. He'd been having too good a time bouncing from one thing to another like the *Sea-Rover* hitting the crests.

"Well, what's wrong with that?" he argued crossly with himself. "It's summer and we're supposed to have a good time. So what if we've been fighting? That can be a good time too, till somebody messes it up."

The trouble was, he wasn't sure who had messed this fight up. First he blamed Uncle Steve for coming along when he did. Then, in some crazy way that he couldn't understand, he blamed Enos and Lewis. That wasn't sensible either.

When he reached the other gate, he saw Eric coming from the house to meet him. Their greetings were silent, a stiff lift of Eric's hand, a hunch of Jamie's shoulder. Their faces were grimly blank. They cut down across the meadow toward the cove, and didn't speak until they had reached the edge of the bank. Then, as if the same signal had been given to each at the same moment, they turned to each other and spoke at the same time.

"I don't care what you—"

"I've been thinking—"

They stopped short and burst out laughing. It was a tremendous relief, as if they'd been under a strain for a long time. Then they sobered, and Jamie reached down and picked a strand of sweet grass and began to chew it. "What were you going to say?"

"What were *you* going to say?"

"I've been thinking we got things to talk over," said Jamie.

Eric looked at him steadily. "I don't want to fight with the MacKenzies any more. I'll have to if you want to keep it up, because we're all for one and one for all. But I don't want to."

"I don't guess I want to, either," admitted Jamie, and they grinned sheepishly at each other. "But we can't let 'em go on hauling our traps! And they don't even *wait* for us to start something, they do it first!"

"Let's go down to our fishhouse and talk," said Eric. "First thing you know somebody'll want me for something." As they started along he said, "Look, put it all together. The way they act and what we know about them now."

"Boy, is that Lewis a sneak," said Jamie.

"Yeah, but if he hadn't listened we'd still be thinking the MacKenzies were just plain ugly customers. Now we know what they've got to be ugly about. How would *you* like it if your father was in jail?" Eric's eyes blazed. "He *killed* someone. My gosh, what if you thought your father was the greatest guy in the world and he does something like that and gets tossed in prison?"

"I don't know how it would be," Jamie said huskily, "because I just can't figure it. My father wouldn't do anything like that any more than yours would."

"Just the same it could happen," Eric argued. "How many guys guess their father's going to get killed? Of course I was too little to guess anything when it happened to my father, but I thought about it afterwards. I used to think all the time, 'Why did it have to happen to *my* father? Other kids' fathers came back from the war all right. Why did I have to lose mine?' Boy, I thought about it all the time."

Jamie listened to him with respect.

"Well," Eric went on, "for the MacKenzies it's just the same as if their father's dead, only it's worse, because he's not a hero. Maybe he still is a hero to *them,* if they don't believe he did anything wrong, but he's not a hero to anybody else."

"But we didn't even know their father was in jail."

"How do they know that? They think everybody knows about it. And they think about it all the time."

"I'd never plague anybody for what their father did," Jamie said furiously.

"But they don't know that."

They lapsed into silence as they walked around the

shore. Jamie was trying with all his might to imagine himself in the MacKenzies' shoes. It was hard, but he concentrated until his head felt light. And soon he had a faint but very painful idea what it would be like to have his father in jail.

"It must be some awful to be on relief!" he burst out. "Having to take charity from folks you think despise you!"

"So you're going to despise them first, see?" said Eric.

Jamie saw. "No wonder they keep going in that old sieve, trying to earn what money they can," he mused. "Know what? I can almost see why they hauled our traps. But—" He shook his head and looked solemnly at Eric. "We can't let 'em keep on doing it, you know. After all, we've got our bills to pay. And besides, they might end up in real bad trouble, starting out like that."

"Sure, we've got to stop 'em," Eric agreed. "But how?"

They brooded on that awhile. Then Jamie said slowly, "If they had some decent traps . . ."

"And a decent boat to get around in," added Eric. "Gorry!" he burst out. "If only anybody could get any-where near them without them bringing out the artil-lery!"

"And even if they let you talk, they'd probably think you were insulting them. Well, try never was beat. Maybe we better rig up a white flag and come a-waving it." They grinned at each other. "Would you really lend the peapod?"

"I would if you would. Of course," Eric added prac-tically, "they'd be likely to take better care of it if they had to pay rent, and then they wouldn't think it was charity, either."

"We-ell..." Jamie looked off into space for a long time. It was a hard decision to make. They were approaching the clump of spruces that hid the fishhouse. Jamie was walking ahead. He looked back over his shoulder at Eric and said, "What if they say yes, sure, thanks, just so they can get ahold of the peapod and smash her up?"

He didn't get any answer. Eric was looking past him with an expression of amazement and horror on his face. Jamie felt that fist in his stomach again, turned slowly, and beheld the ruins of their fishhouse.

All the time they'd spent in wheeling, lugging, lifting, and nailing, had come to this—a heap of rubble. The old boards had been split and pulled off; the door was flung to one side with ax blows through its weathered panels; broken glass from the windows glinted among the mosses. Spare buoys and tools were flung everywhere, and rope festooned the entire mess.

The boys stared with round eyes, their throats dry. It was Eric who spoke first. "What in heck did they use?" he muttered in awe. "Axes, wrecking bars? Gosh, if they'd just smashed the windows and pulled the door off! But this is—this is—"

"Look," said Jamie. He said it very quietly because he felt so quiet. All the rage the MacKenzies had caused in him so far built up to one enormous hush. He pointed to a board that had been pulled off almost whole. Along the length of it there was a message in red buoy paint.

"The MacKenzies were here," it said.

Eric sat down on a rock and gazed at the message. "So they're the ones we had all these boy scout ideas about," he said bitterly. "Now I'd never let 'em get within fifty feet of the peapod!"

Jamie narrowed his eyes and spoke in sharp biting words. "You know what they did? When Uncle Steve hauled us off this morning, they stayed right there and must have gone ashore as soon as we were out of sight. Went rampaging through the woods and saw our fish-house and—"

"They must have gone up to the house when they saw nobody was home," said Eric. "They must've got the axes and the wrecking bar from the workshop."

Jamie said coldly, "I s'pose we should be thankful they didn't bother to set fire to the island. They must be saving that for next time."

He squinted at the message again. "Proud of themselves, aren't they? Don't want anybody else to get the credit for the job. Well, come on." He got up.

"Come on *where?*" Eric said curtly.

"This time we're not stopping to look around, we're going right up to the door and ask 'em what in heck's the idea, and if they want a fight to the finish we'll have one."

"Whose finish?" Eric inquired, but he got up too.

They walked rapidly up to the harbor. Jamie felt as if he could fly if he tried, he was so angry. It was a good feeling, as if nothing or nobody could get in his way.

"If we don't get over there and settle this today, I'll

bust," Jamie muttered. "I bet they're laughing themselves sick right now about what they did."

Eric was pale, as he always was under emotion. "This was going to be a swell summer," he said. "Oh boy, it sure is. Swell for somebody."

"It *is* a swell summer," Jamie protested.

"Boy, you sure like to fight. I can tell you're descended from those Vikings, all right."

The boat touched the shore. Jamie wound the line around the post and they went down the beach. "Listen," he said quietly as he untied the painter. "You don't have to go, see? It just happens to be *our* fishhouse they wrecked, but if you don't want to go I'll go alone."

"You will if you get out of the harbor," Eric said with a touch of his usual humor. "Who said I wanted to stay home? I may not go around yelling war cries, but I'm just as mad as you are."

Jamie grinned. "Let's go, then. And don't look over toward the store. If they see us acting furtive, they'll be suspicious. Right now they think we're going fishing in the harbor, or something."

Eric got in, Jamie pushed off and climbed in over the bow. Eric started the engine, and they swung out toward the harbor mouth. Neither of them looked back at the shore. If they didn't actually *see* anyone waving them back, it would come in handy if there was any trouble with parents afterward. And of course they couldn't *hear* anything over the engine.

16 Green Apple Storm

It was choppy in the harbor and the *Sea-Rover* bounced like a chip, but once they were outside, they were more or less in the lee all the way, except for a rather heavy swash around Tenpound. They went by the ledges that guarded the entrance to Brigport harbor, and soon were running down the northern side. Here the water lay flat and calm in the deserted little coves, and the sun was very warm after the cold brisk wind on the other side.

After they shut off the engine and landed, the quietness seemed unnatural. Eric went over the rocks and looked to see if the dory was there—it was. The boys exchanged tense grins and started up through the alder-grown pasture. It was very hot and they were sweating by the time they came out to where the cellar hole was.

The boys had been walking briskly, but they came to a stop at the road as if it were a deep and rushing current. They looked and listened. Nothing moved around the old gray house and the ramshackle barn looming behind it. No wind touched the leaves of the ancient apple trees or the spruce boughs of the surrounding woods. Everything seemed to be asleep, or waiting.

"Looks as if nobody's home," Eric whispered. "Maybe they've all gone somewhere. Berrying, or haying for somebody."

Jamie kept his eyes on the house. "I've got a feeling they're right there," he answered. "Maybe watching us."

"Well, we'll know if a bullet whistles by our ears," Eric said with a faint attempt at humor. Neither boy moved. For all his earlier eagerness, Jamie felt as if his feet were glued to the ground.

Then all at once there was a sharp fast knocking in the silence, and both boys jumped, stared wildly at each other, and then burst into laughter which they hastily subdued. "Woodpecker," said Eric. "Something alive around here, anyway."

"He gave me an idea," said Jamie. "Let's walk straight up and knock on the door."

Stiffening their shoulders, they strode across the road under the apple trees. Their stride was somewhat spoiled by the hard green apples that rolled under their feet, but they kept on going as if to stop would be fatal. Shoulder to shoulder they reached the front doorstep and stepped up on it. Jamie knocked. There was no sound from inside the house, and Eric whispered, "Nobody's home."

"It looks as if nobody's used this door for years," said Jamie. "Nailed shut, likely. Let's try the kitchen door."

They went along the length of the house to the ell, and Eric poked Jamie violently in the ribs and pointed. In the jog between house and ell was a small but rich flower bed, exactly the same as their mothers had. They had other garden beds and borders, but the little corner of old-fashioned flowers watered by dish water always grew brightest and best of all.

For an instant the boys looked at the garden, which definitely proved that the MacKenzies had a mother who was like anyone else's mother. Then Jamie snorted, "Bet she has to stand guard over it with a club. They'd likely tramp it down just for fun." He went up on the step and knocked sharply, like the woodpecker.

Again there was no answer. This door had a screen door and he tried to see through it, but the kitchen was dim after all the sunshine outdoors.

"They're somewhere around here!" he said angrily. "We'll just wait till they show up, then!"

At that moment Jeannie and young Laddie came around the corner of the barn. They didn't see the boys at first. Jeannie wore an apron over her faded shorts and a boy's shirt. She was carrying a small basket.

"See, I told you," she said to Laddie. "I *told* you Blackie would lay an egg for your birthday cake."

"Yes, but how did she know it was my birthday?"

Jeannie smiled at him. "Because I told her yesterday, silly. I asked her to lay two if she could, and she said she'd do her best, on account of you're her favorite Mac-Kenzie. But she couldn't lay two, so she asked Old Lady Henrietta to help out."

"And now we're going to make the cake!" sang Laddie, and skipped with joy.

Jeannie began to sing his words to the tune of *The Farmer in the Dell,* and he joined in, and so they came happily toward the house.

144

"We're going to make a cake,
    We're going to make a cake,
    Laddie's going to fetch the wood,
    While Jeannie makes the cake."

With the last word on their lips they saw the boys on the doorstep. Jeannie's face went blank and still. Laddie was too excited to see them as enemies.

"It's my birthday!" he cried. "I'm six today!"

"That's swell," said Eric. "Gosh, already you're a lot taller than you were yesterday."

"Don't you talk to him!" snapped Jeannie. "And you get out of here quick!"

"You can't drive us," said Jamie, "because you haven't got your gun. Anyway, we don't fight with girls or little kids."

"You're some noble," said Jeannie scornfully. "Let me by, then. I've got work to do. You start fetching your wood, Laddie." She went into the house. She tried to slam the screen door but it swung open again, creaking mournfully. When she came back to close it she gave the boys an icy, slit-eyed stare.

"Can I have a drink?" Jamie asked with suspicious meekness.

"*No!*" She went away from the door and they soon heard the rattle of stove covers. Laddie filled his arms at the chopping block until he could hardly see over the load, and pieces kept falling off.

"Let's help him," Jamie said, winking at Eric. "Here,

give us some of that, Laddie. We'll help fill your wood-box and you can hold the door open for us."

Laddie thought that was fine. "Bruce and Robbie and Jeannie don't like you," he told them earnestly, "but I do." He ran ahead to open the door, singing out, "We've got lots of wood, Jeannie!"

Jeannie clattered a stove cover back into place and help-lessly ordered them out. They ignored her and filled the woodbox. "Now can we have a drink, ma'am?" Jamie mocked her.

Laddie cried, "The water's in here!" and led the way to the pantry.

Jamie noticed how bare and clean everything was. The floors and cupboards looked as if they'd been scrubbed down to the grain of the wood and the uncurtained win-dows shone. The old black sink in the pantry was wiped dry and clean like the old black range in the kitchen. The water pail from which he drank cold spring water was kept covered with a clean cheesecloth. The house smelled of cleanliness and of flowers which were placed all over in jars and old pitchers.

"Thank you for the water," Eric said politely to Jean-nie, who shrugged her shoulders and began to measure flour.

"Now you can get out," she called to them. "You've seen all there is to see; that's what you came for, isn't it?"

"No," said Jamie. "We came over to have a showdown and we're going to have it. You guys started it and we're going to finish it."

"Oh, you *are!*" She came out of the pantry. "How did we start it?"

"You know. You were there," said Eric. "We wanted to say 'Hi,' and be decent, and you all started yelling at us."

"What about the time when you tried to keep them from taking that bashed-in old trap—you, with your new traps and money to build more, and your fathers running a couple hundred traps apiece!"

"We *didn't* try to keep them from taking it," Eric began patiently, but Jamie interrupted.

"Don't waste your breath on her. Come on outdoors and wait. It's getting hot in here."

Jeannie flung back her head and said dramatically. "It'll be a lot hotter yet when the boys come home! And you stay in here with me, Laddie!" she ordered the little boy, who looked disappointed.

Jamie and Eric turned toward the door, and then stopped. Bruce and Robbie were coming by the flower garden and up onto the doorstep. They'd been sweating, and their damp skin and hair were scattered with spruce spills. They had hatchets in their belts. Jamie guessed that they'd been out in the woods cutting spruce limbs to make bows for lobster pots.

They looked thirsty and tired. They also looked lean, springy, and fierce. Bruce came in first, and when he saw Jamie and Eric in the kitchen he was completely bewildered, but only for a moment.

"What are they doing here?" he demanded of Jeannie.

"They just filled the woodbox so Jeannie can make my birthday cake!" cried Laddie.

"*I* didn't ask 'em to," said Jeannie. "I've told 'em to get out about ten times. But they're waiting for you. They want a showdown."

"We'll give 'em a showdown." Robbie pushed forward like an arrogant young red rooster.

"We aren't having any kind of chew with them," Bruce said. "They're getting out *now*, or I'll kick them out, and that's the end of it."

"Oh, yeah?" flared Jamie. "Well, what if we sneak over here sometime and wreck something the way you wrecked our fishhouse?"

There was a sharp ringing snap against a window behind him. He swung around, and they all looked where he looked. "What was that?" someone said.

"Sounded like a BB," Eric suggested.

"If you two have brought some friends over—" Bruce reached out as if to collar Jamie, who dodged.

"We came alone," he said in disgust. There was another sharp spat. This time Eric looked out and caught a flicker of movement behind a big thick pine at the edge of the woods.

"He's out there," he said. "Somebody with an air rifle." At the same time another BB hit the pantry window.

"More than one!" Robbie shouted. "I'm going out, and—"

Bruce pulled him back. "You want a BB shot in your

ear or your eye? Listen!" There'd been another one, on the window of the third side of the kitchen. He bit the inside of his cheek. "There's a crowd of 'em. Must've come up from the harbor."

"Lewis Fowler's got an air rifle," young Laddie spoke up. "I saw it when I was there with Mama yesterday. He brought it with him, but his grandpa don't let him use it."

"Well, I'm willing to bet he's using it today," Bruce said grimly. "There's some others on here too. Have to be, unless he's flying around the house on wings."

"We've got something better than an air rifle," Jeannie declared. She grabbed a chair to climb up on and get the rifle from where it hung, but Bruce pulled the chair away from her.

"Don't talk so foolish, Jeannie! The way you go for that gun, anybody'd think you were Annie Oakley. We got to think of something else besides that. If we don't, they'll keep us penned up in here all afternoon."

"They'll get tired of that after a while," said Jamie. "No excitement if they can't see anything moving around here. Whaddya bet they start creeping in closer with something else to throw, like rocks or—"

"And what do we throw back?" muttered Bruce. "I almost feel like firing that .22 over their heads and giving 'em a good scare."

"Sure, and get arrested for it," said Jamie. "If that Lewis Fowler's in on this, he'd be yelling bloody murder all over Brigport. It's all he's waiting for. For you to do something he can screech about and maybe put you in jail."

"Besides," said Eric, "what we want is a good fast offensive. Throw a lot of stuff so fast and hard that they can't get through it." He grinned. "The way we did yesterday before my father barged in."

The MacKenzies looked at him suspiciously. He stopped smiling and said, "Got any potatoes in the house? We could throw those."

Jeannie said, "We've got about five. Mama's bringing some home today. We ought to have plenty by and by from the garden—" She gasped and put her hand over her mouth. "They could ruin my garden!"

"Not if we see them first," said Jamie.

"*We?*" Bruce scowled at him. "This isn't your fight."

"Well, we're stuck with it," said Jamie. "You don't suppose they care who's in here, do you?"

"Green apples!" cried Eric triumphantly. "Out under the trees!"

"Ayuh, they came down in the wind a while back," said Robbie.

"And they're on the side nobody's fired at—yet," said Jamie. "You guys watch the windows from in here, so they can't sneak up on us, and I'll go out a window and load up. Gimme something to carry them in."

Jeannie dumped the drinking water into a kettle and produced another pail from the cellar way. "I'll show you where you can get out," she said. "The front door's nailed shut. We had to, to keep the rain out."

She led the way through the house to the end where the apple trees were. She took the sliding screen out of the window and held the sash up for him to climb out. When he landed on the ground she handed out the pails.

Crouching low, but still feeling painfully exposed, he ran for the apple trees and began filling the pails as fast as he could.

"Hey, Jamie!" a voice hailed him from close by. His head flew up, and he saw Enos Pearce pressed close to the side of the barn.

"What do you want?" Jamie growled and went on picking apples. So in another moment they'd nick him with their BB's. Well, he wasn't going to run for it and get stung on the seat.

"I didn't know you was friends with *them,*" Enos went on.

"I'm not." Jamie resisted an impulse to lob a hard apple at Enos.

"Eric with you?"

"What business is it of yours?"

"What are you gathering them green apples for?"

"A pie," snarled Jamie.

"Well, listen," said Enos. "Lewis says we'll give you time to clear out of here, so you better go while you can. It's going to be real rough. There's eleven of us, and we aren't going back to the harbor till the MacKenzies know we've been here."

Jamie sat back on his heels and glared openly in Enos's direction, and now for the first time he saw the big vegetable garden laid out between the barn and the woods. The garden must have been dug up by hand. Ayuh, he thought savagely, and I'll bet those low-lifes have tramped half of it down already!

"You tell Ol' Sneaky Lewis," he said, "that he's been watching too many TV shows." He got up then, picked up his full buckets and walked to the house, fully expecting to hear the crack of an air rifle behind him. But Enos was a little slow on the trigger, and the BB cracked into a clapboard beside him as he handed the buckets over the sill to Jeannie and climbed in after them.

She was pale under her freckles. "Why don't you and Eric go while you can?" she asked breathlessly. "It's not your fight."

"Sure it is," said Jamie. "We came looking for a fight and we're going to have one." He would have swaggered except that the buckets were so heavy.

"Eleven of 'em," he reported in the kitchen. "Bunch of dopey ginks with nothing to do, so they go out and start up a war."

A rock struck the side of the house from inside the big open barn doorway. "There's a little door at the back of the barn," Bruce said tightly. "They've come in that way."

"They won't hurt Blackie, will they?" cried Laddie. "Or ol' Lady Henrietta?"

"Of course not," said Jeannie crossly, but growing paler. "They're just mad with us, not with hens."

Behind her a window shattered—rock and glass flew

into the kitchen. Bruce reached Laddie in one stride and hoisted the little boy onto the stairs that ran up one side of the kitchen wall. "You stay up on them steps, and don't you move, you hear me?" he said fiercely. "The rest of you, stay away from them windows. We'll let them do their best and come real close, and then we'll let them have it."

They pressed back against the walls while the rocks beat against the sides of the house, while more glass crashed in the other rooms. Nobody spoke. Their eyes were quick, their mouths tight. They were waiting until the others would be drawn by curiosity to converge on the house to find out why nobody was striking back.

In the kitchen, pressed against the walls, the besieged ones seemed hardly to breathe. They waited until the last one had crept so close that he wouldn't be able to get back to the barn's shelter quickly enough to protect himself. The invaders gathered in a little knot in the dooryard, staring curiously and uneasily at the house.

"*Now!*" Bruce said softly, and they streamed out of the door, forcefully hurling their apples into the group. The answering yelps and squawks were music to their ears. Jeannie came behind with the supply buckets.

The enemy made a few efforts to salvage some of the rocks they'd thrown at the house, but hard green apples making contact spoiled the attempt. Some had a handful of rocks left, and threw them, but the green apples came so thick and fast that a couple of the fighters broke and ran for the road.

One straggler came around the corner of the house with his air rifle, raised it and aimed it. With a yell of triumph Robbie flung an apple that struck the barrel, knocking the gun out of the owner's hands. Lewis, having dropped his under the first artillery attack, pounced on this one and received a hard shower of apples on the back of his head. He came up yelling and brandishing the rifle.

"Jailbirds!" he shouted. "You'll all be jailbirds just like your old man!"

"Jailbirds, jailbirds!" a few of the others took up the cry, dodging apples or yiping when one made contact, throwing them back when they could. Jamie saw Enos

Pearse running for the road, smiled scornfully, and then lobbed an especially large and very hard apple straight at Lewis's open mouth.

Lewis yelped and clapped his hand to a bleeding lip. Into this scene of havoc came Mr. Fowler's jeep, bringing Mrs. MacKenzie home.

The defenders, backed against the ell wall, saw the jeep first. But Lewis didn't see it. Infuriated by the blow on his mouth, he yelled, "I know all about your father! I know why you have to live on charity! I know——"

Mr. Fowler's face, which had seemed to Jamie a fairly ordinary face, had an extraordinary expression as he walked over the grass behind Lewis. Mrs. MacKenzie hurried toward the house. She was a neat, rather pretty woman, who looked frightened.

Lewis saw her and his shouts started to die. Then his grandfather touched him on the shoulder and Lewis whirled around.

"Grandpa!" he yipped.

"Into the jeep," said his grandfather, tight-lipped. "The rest of you, *git!*"

Those who hadn't run before ran now. Lewis hurried to the jeep. Mr. Fowler came over to the ell, walking carefully among the green apples and stones.

"I'll get Lewis's story when I get home," he said quietly. "I'd like yours now.—Whatever it is, I intend to take up with him the remarks he was making when we drove into the yard. Believe me, Emmie, he never heard those things from me."

"I know that, Ralph." She gave him a slight smile. "But oh—this house—the windows—" She shook her head and her eyes filled with tears.

"Are you boys ready to give me a story?" Mr. Fowler asked them sternly. Jeannie had ducked around the corner; Laddie had come out and was hanging onto his mother. Bruce and Robbie stood very straight, their red hair like crests, and looked back silently at Mr. Fowler. He shook his head, then turned to Jamie and Eric.

"You'd be doing me a great favor if you'd tell me the truth. I know your families, and I know you boys aren't troublemakers. You've got to have a good reason for being here."

"We came over on business," said Eric. Jamie swallowed and picked up the cue. There was no chance to talk it over privately. He could only hope he and Eric were thinking together.

"Eric and I have been talking about letting these kids rent our peapod," he said boldly. That was no lie, he thought. We *had* talked about it before they wrecked our fishhouse.

"And they can get some second-hand traps from my father too," Eric put in. "They're all right for summer-time fishing."

"See, we were in the kitchen, talking about—about the fishhouse Eric and I built, when somebody fired an air rifle at the window," Jamie said. "That's how it started."

Mr. Fowler studied him. "I see," he said finally. "Well, Bruce, I'm glad to see that you're looking ahead

156

and showing some ambition. I want to have a talk with you before long about your plans. Every time I mention it, you flinch away like I tunked you with a red hot poker. You've got to get over that nonsense. You've got your way to make in the world and a family to take care of for a while yet." He turned to Mrs. MacKenzie.

"Emmie," he said sternly, "I'll send somebody up with some glass and putty as soon as I get back to the harbor. Lewis and the other boys in this thing will pay for it before the summer's out. Lewis is going to work for me in the store from now on." He nodded curtly at them all, and started back to the jeep.

When he had gone, Jamie said to Eric, "Well, let's go."

Jeannie came rushing around the corner. "They *did* walk through my garden and they stepped on some turnips and beets, but—hey, are you going?"

"Yep," said Jamie.

"Well, don't you want a drink of water first?"

"You mean you're *offering* it?" said Eric, and they all laughed.

Mrs. MacKenzie smiled anxiously at Jamie and Eric. "It's good of you to let Bruce rent the peapod. That dory's such a hard old thing to manage, and its so leaky."

"Well, listen," Bruce began, then swallowed hard and turned a different red from the color of his hair. "You guys—what's the idea? After we—" He stopped short.

"Come on," Jamie said again to Eric.

"We'll walk down to the shore with you," said Bruce grimly. "Don't touch that glass, Mother. We'll clean it up." When they had crossed the road, he said in a low savage voice, "What's the idea? After we wrecked your fishhouse and all?"

"We didn't come over to offer you the rent of the pea-pod, you know that," said Eric. "But we were *going* to offer it, before we saw what you did to the fishhouse."

"Honest," Jamie grumbled, "you're so stiff-necked, you don't even wait to see if anybody wants to be friends or not. That day you lugged the trap off, we were going to tell you about those traps of Uncle Steve's——"

Robbie burst out, "What about us hauling your traps that time? Don't ever tell our mother, will you?"

"We never told anybody," said Jamie. "But we didn't plan to let you get away with it. That's why we hauled yours."

"And don't tell our fathers, will you?" Eric broke in with a grin. "We're in enough trouble now."

Jamie went on.

"We just wanted to warn you. Look, if you have some decent traps and some decent bait, you ought to do all right and not have to haul anybody else."

"We never meant to keep on doing it, and we don't need to be preached at." Bruce glared at Jamie. "And while we're throwing cold facts around—our father never killed anybody on purpose in his life. It was an accident, and they called it manslaughter. And he'll be out in two years, and he's coming here, and we want something decent for him to come to."

"Sure you do," said Eric sympathetically. Jamie nodded sternly. Bruce kept on glaring.

"And we'll help you build up that foolish shack again, too."

"O.K.," said Jamie in a matter-of-fact tone. "Come over and get the peapod when you're ready."

"And see my father about the pots," Eric added. They started down toward the boat.

"Wait a minute, wait a minute!" Jeannie came running down through the alders, flushed with heat and excitement, her eyes shining. She was pretty now that she wasn't taut with rage. "What was it you wanted out of the old cellar hole? Aren't you going to take it while we're all speaking?"

"Guess I better," Jamie admitted. "Can't tell how these touchy MacKenzies'll be tomorrow."

They all laughed, Jeannie whole-heartedly, Robbie with reluctance that gradually gave way to enthusiasm, and Bruce beginning with a slow smile that turned at last into a grin. In that instant Jamie realized that some time ago he'd ceased to regard them as sworn enemies. It began to look as if it might be a good summer after all.

Tired, contented, feeling as if they had made a long but highly successful journey together in the last hour, the five walked up through the pasture toward the cellar hole.

Local and Lobstering Terms

Buoy	The wooden float that marks the location of the lobster trap. Each fisherman has his own colors for his buoys.
Chop	A slight roughness to the water.
Double-ender *Peapod*	Two words for the same thing. A rowboat which is shaped exactly the same at both ends. (Something like a peapod after the peas have been taken out.) Of light construction.
Fog mull	A long spell of fog.
Funny-eye	A traphead has a hole in the middle for the lobsters to crawl through in search of the bait in the trap. The hole is held open by a hoop called a funny-eye.
High-liner	The man who is getting the most lobsters.
Lobster car	A float with compartments, water-filled, in which lobsters are stored. A buyer has a big car, with weighing scales on it, where he buys the lobsterman's catch.
Mug-up	A snack. (From the fisherman's habit of drinking tea or coffee from a mug.)
Pot	Another word for lobster trap.
Traphead	The specially shaped twine net that fills in each end of a lobster trap. These days most trapheads are made of nylon twine.
Warp	The special rope which leads from the buoy to the trap.